Mary Poppins

in Cherry Tree Lane

*Have you read all the original
Mary Poppins adventures?*

Mary Poppins

Mary Poppins
Comes Back

Mary Poppins
Opens the Door

Mary Poppins
in the Park

Mary Poppins
in Cherry Tree Lane

Mary Poppins
and the House Next Door

Mary Poppins
in Cherry Tree Lane

P. L. TRAVERS

Illustrated by Mary Shepard

HarperCollins *Children's Books*

Mary Poppins in Cherry Tree Lane first published in Great Britain
by William Collins Sons & Co Ltd. 1982
Mary Poppins and the House Next Door first published in Great Britain
by William Collins Sons & Co Ltd. 1988
Two-in-one edition first published by HarperCollins *Children's Books* 1988
This edition published by HarperCollins *Children's Books* 2016
HarperCollins *Children's Books* is a division of HarperCollins*Publishers* Ltd,
1 London Bridge Street, London SE1 9GF

The HarperCollins *Children's Books* website address is
www.harpercollins.co.uk

12

Text copyright © The Trustees of the P.L. Travers Will Trust 1982, 1988
Illustrations copyright © Mary Shepard 1982, 1988

P.L. Travers and Mary Shepard assert the moral right
to be identified as the author and illustrator of this work.

ISBN 978-0-00-820746-5

Printed and bound in England by
CPI Group (UK) Ltd, Croydon, CR0 4YY

CONTENTS

To KLT and CJT

It was Midsummer's Eve. This is the most magical night of the year. Many curious things can happen in it before it gives way to the dawn. But it was not night yet by any means. The sun, still bright, was dawdling to the west, lazily taking his time about it, as though reluctant to leave the world.

He felt that he had done it proud, putting upon it a shine and a polish that would not quickly fade. His own reflection shone back at him from fountains, lakes and window-panes, even from the ripened fruit that hung in the trees of Cherry Tree Lane, a place well known to him.

"Nothing like sunshine," he flattered himself, as he noted the glitter of the ship's lanterns on either side of the Admiral's gate; the sparkle of the brass knocker on the door of Miss Lark's mansion; the gleam that came from an old tin toy, abandoned, apparently, by its owners, in the garden of the smallest house. This too, was a place well known to him.

"Not a soul in sight," he thought to himself, as he sent his long light over the Lane and then across the open space, large and green and blossoming, that spread beside and beyond it. And this too, he knew well. After all, he had had a hand in its making. For where would they be – tree, grass and flower – without, as it were, his helping hand, greening the grass, coaxing the leaf from the bare bough, warming the bud into flower?

And here, among lengthening light and shadows, there *was* a soul in sight.

"Who's that, down there in the Park?" he wondered, as a curious figure went back and forth, blowing a whistle and shouting.

Who else could it be but the Park Keeper? It was no wonder, however, that the sun did not recognise him for, in spite of the heavy heat of June, he was wearing a black, felt, sea-faring hat painted with skull-and-crossbones.

"Obey the Rules! Remember the Bye-laws! All Litter to be placed in the Baskets!" he bellowed.

But nobody took any notice. People went strolling hand in hand; scattering litter as they went; deliberately sauntering on lawns whose notices said KEEP OFF THE GRASS; failing to Observe the Rules; forgetting all the Bye-laws.

The Policeman was marching to and fro, swinging his baton and looking important, as if he thought he owned the earth and expected the earth to be glad of it.

Children went up and down on the swings, swooping like evening swallows.

And the swallows sang their songs so loudly that nobody heard the Park Keeper's whistle.

Admiral and Mrs Boom, sharing a bag of peanuts between them and dropping the empty shells as they went, were taking the air in the Long Walk.

> "Oh, I'm roaming
> In the gloaming
> with my lassie by my side!"

sang the Admiral, disregarding the signboard's warning No HAWKERS, NO MUSICIANS.

In the Rose Garden, a tall man, in a cricketing cap a little too small and skimpy for him, was dipping his handkerchief into the fountain and was mopping his sunburnt brow.

Down by the Lake, an elderly gentleman in a hat of folded newspaper stood turning his head this way and that, sniffing the air like a gun dog.

"Coo-ee, Professor!" called Miss Lark, hurrying across the lawns, with her dogs unwillingly dragging behind her, as though they wished they were somewhere else.

For Miss Lark, to celebrate Midsummer's Eve, had tied a ribbon upon each head – pink for Willoughby, blue for Andrew – and they felt ashamed and dejected. What, they wondered, would people think? They might be mistaken for poodles!

"Professor, I've been waiting for you. You must have lost your way."

"Well, that's the way with ways, I suppose. Either you lose them or they lose you. Anyway, you've found me, Miss

Sparrow. But, alas!" he fanned himself with his hat, "I find the Sahara Desert a little – er – hot."

"You are not in the Sahara, Professor. You are in the Park. Don't you remember? I invited you to supper."

"Ah, so you did. To Strawberry Street. I hope it will be cooler there. For you and me and your two – um – poodles."

Andrew and Willoughby hung their heads. Their worst fears had been realised.

"No, no. The address is Cherry Tree Lane. And my name is Lucinda Lark. Do try not to be so forgetful. Ah, there you are, dear friends!" she trilled, as she spied the Booms in the distance. "Where are you off to this beautiful evening?"

"Sailing, sailing, over a bounding main," sang the Admiral. "And many a stormy wind shall blow, till Jack comes home again – won't it, messmate?" he enquired of his wife.

"Yes, dear," murmured Mrs Boom. "Unless you would like to wait till tomorrow. Binnacle is making Cottage Pie and there will be Apple Tart for dinner."

"Cottage Pie! I can't miss that. Let down the anchor, midshipman. We'll wait for the morning tide."

"Yes, dear," Mrs Boom agreed. But she knew there would be no morning tide. She also knew that the Admiral, although he was always talking about it, would never go to sea again. It was far too far away from land and it always made him seasick.

"Obey the Rules! Observe the Bye-laws!" The Park Keeper rushed past, blowing his whistle.

"Ship ahoy there! Heave to, old salt!" The Admiral seized the Park Keeper's sleeve. "That's my hat you're wearing, skipper. I won it in a hand-to-hand fight off the coast of Madagascar. Didn't I, messmate?" he demanded.

"If you say so, dear," murmured Mrs Boom. It was better, she knew, to agree than to argue. But privately she was aware of the facts – that the hat belonged to Binnacle, a retired pirate who kept the Admiral's ship-shaped house as shipshape as only a pirate could; and, moreover, that neither he nor her husband had ever clapped eyes on Madagascar.

"And I thought I had lost my Skull-and-Crossbones! Where did you find it, you son of a sea-snake?"

"Well, it fell down, sort of, out of the sky." The Park Keeper shuffled uneasily. "And I put it on by mistake, so to say, not meaning any harm, Admiral, sir."

"Nonsense! You're thinking of cannon balls. Pirate hats don't fall from the sky. Hand it over to Mrs Boom. She carries all the heavy things while I spy out the land." The Admiral took out his telescope and fixed it to his eye.

"But what am I going to put on my head?" the Park Keeper demanded.

"Go to sea, my man, and they'll give you a cap. A white thing with HMS Something on it. You can't have my pirate hat, I need it. For away I'm bound to go – oho! – 'cross the wide Missouri."

And the Admiral, singing lustily, dragged his wife and the hat away.

The Park Keeper glanced round anxiously. What if the Lord Mayor came along and found him with his head uncovered? He dared not think of the consequences. If only the long day were over. If only all these crowding people, lolling or strolling hand in hand, would go home to their suppers. Then he could lock the Park Gates and slip away into the dark where his lack of a cap would not be noticed. If only the sun would go down!

But the sun still lingered. No one went home. They merely opened paper bags, took out cakes and sandwiches and threw the bags on to the grass.

"You'd think they thought they owned the Park," said the Park Keeper, who thought he owned it himself.

More people streamed in through the Main Gate, two by two, choosing balloons; or two by two from Mudge's Fair Ground, buying ice cream from the Ice Cream Man, each one holding the other's hand as the falling sun threw their long shadows before them on the lawns.

And then, through the Lane Gate, came another shadow that preceded through the two pillars a small but formal procession – a perambulator packed with toys and children; at one side a girl who carried a basket, at the other a boy in a sailor suit with a string bag swinging from his hand.

Basket and bag were both well stocked as though for some lengthy excursion. And, pushing the perambulator, was an upright figure with bright pink cheeks, bright blue eyes and a turned-up nose – a figure that to the Park Keeper was only too familiar.

"Oh, *no!*" he muttered to himself. "Not at this hour, for Heaven's sake! What's she doing setting out when she ought to be going home?"

He crossed the lawn and accosted the group.

"Late, aren't you?" he enquired, trying, as far as he could, to look friendly. If he had been some kind of dog, his tail would have given a modest wag.

"Late for what?" Mary Poppins demanded, looking right through the Park Keeper as though he were a window.

He quailed visibly. "Well, what I meant to say was – you're sort of upside down, so to speak."

The blue eyes grew a shade bluer. He could see he had offended her.

"Are you accusing me," she enquired, "a well-brought-up respectable person, of standing on my head?"

"No, no, of course not. Not on your head. Not like an acrobat. Nothing like that."

The Park Keeper, thoroughly muddled, was now afraid that he himself was the one that was upside down.

"It's just that it's sort of late in the day, the time when you're usually coming back – tea and bed and that sort of thing. And here you are, sallying forth, as though you were off on a jaunt." He eyed the bulging bag and basket. "With all and sundry, so to speak."

"We are. We're having a supper picnic." Jane pointed to the basket. "There's plenty of everything in here. You never know when a friend will appear – so Mary Poppins says."

"And we're staying up for hours and hours," said Michael, swinging his bag.

"*A supper picnic!*" The Park Keeper winced. He had never heard of such a thing. And was it even permitted, he wondered.

His list of Bye-laws raced through his head and he promptly gave it tongue.

"Observe the Rules!" he warned the group. "All Litter to be placed in the proper containers. No eggshells left lying about on the grass."

"Are we cuckoos," demanded Mary Poppins, "to be scattering eggs in every direction?"

"I meant hard-boiled," said the Park Keeper. "There never was a picnic, ever, that didn't have hard-boiled eggs. And where are you going, might I ask?" If the picnic was to be in the Park, he felt he had a right to know.

"We're off to—" Jane began eagerly.

"That will do, Jane," said Mary Poppins. "We will not hob-nob with strangers."

"But I'm no stranger!" The Park Keeper stared. "I'm here every day and Sundays. You know me. I'm the Park Keeper."

"Then why aren't you wearing your hat?" she demanded, giving the perambulator such a forceful push that if the Park Keeper had not jumped backwards, it would have run over his foot.

"Step along, please!" said Mary Poppins. And the little cavalcade stepped along, orderly and purposeful.

The Park Keeper watched till it disappeared, with a swish of Mary Poppins' new sprigged dress, behind the rhododendrons.

"Hob-nob!" he spluttered. "Who does she think she is, I wonder?"

There was no one at hand to answer that question and the Park Keeper dismissed it. Uppity – that's what she was, he thought. And no great bargain to look at either. She could go where she liked for all he cared – the Long Walk led to all sorts of places: the Zoo, St Paul's, even the River – it might be any of them. Well, he couldn't patrol the whole of London. His job was to see to the Park. So, ready for any misdemeanour, he cast a vigilant eye about him.

"Hey, you!" he shouted warningly, as the tall man who had washed his face in the fountain bent down to smell a rose – and picked it! "No Picking of Flowers allowed in the Park. Obey the Rules. Remember the Bye-laws!"

"I could hardly forget them," the tall man answered. "Considering I was the one who made them."

"Ha, ha! *You* made them! Very funny!" The Park Keeper laughed a mirthless laugh.

"Well, some of them, I admit, are funny. They often make me chuckle. But, have you forgotten, it's Midsummer's Eve? Nobody keeps the Bye-laws tonight. And I myself don't *have* to keep them, now or at any time."

"Oh, no? And who do you fancy you are then?"

"One doesn't fancy. One just knows. It's the kind of thing one can't forget. I'm the Prime Minister."

The Park Keeper flung back his head and guffawed. "Not in that silly cap, you're not. Prime Ministers wear black shiny hats and white stripes down their trousers."

"Well, I've been having a game of cricket. I know it's too small. I've grown out of it. But you can't wear a top hat when you're batting – or bowling, for that matter."

"I see. And now you've had your little game, you're off to

visit the King, I suppose?" The Park Keeper was sarcastic.

"Well, as a matter of fact, I am. An important letter arrived from the Palace as I was leaving home. Now, where did I put the wretched thing? Drat these skimpy flannel pockets! Not in this one, not in that. Can I have lost it? Ah, now I remember!" He wrenched off the offending cap and took from within it an envelope sealed with a large gold crown.

"DEAR PRIME MINISTER," he read out. "IF YOU HAVE NOTHING BETTER TO DO, PLEASE COME OVER TO DINNER. LOBSTER, TRIFLE, SARDINES ON TOAST. I AM THINKING OF MAKING A FEW NEW LAWS AND WOULD BE SO GLAD OF A CHAT."

"There! What did I tell you? And tonight of all nights! One never gets a moment's peace. I don't mind the chat, that's part of my job. But I can't stand lobster. It upsets my digestion. Oh, well, I'll have to go, I suppose. Bye-laws can always be by-passed, but Laws have to be kept. And anyway," he said haughtily, folding his arms and looking important, "what has it got to do with you? A perfect stranger accosting me and telling me – *me!* – not to pick the roses! That's the Park Keeper's business."

"I-I *am* the Park Keeper," the Park Keeper said, shuddering from head to foot as he stared at the regal letter. He had made a terrible mistake and he trembled to think where it might lead him.

The Prime Minister lifted his monocle, screwed it firmly into his eye and regarded the figure before him.

"*I am shocked!*" he said sombrely. "Even stupefied. Almost, I might say, speechless. A public servant in a public place failing to array himself in the uniform provided! I don't know when I have been so displeased. And what, pray, have you done with your hat?"

"I-I dropped it in a Litter-basket."

"A *Litter*-basket! A receptacle for orange peel! An employee of the County Council who thinks so little of his hat that he throws it into a – well, really! This kind of thing must not go on. It would bring the country to the verge of ruin. I shall speak to the Lord Mayor."

"Oh, please, Your Honour, it just happened. A little slip when my mind was elsewhere. I'll go through the litter tomorrow and find it. Not the Lord Mayor, Your Worship, *please*! Think of my poor old mother."

"You should have thought of her yourself. Park Keepers are paid to think. To keep their minds here, not elsewhere. And not to let things just happen. However, as it is Midsummer's Eve – only once a year, after all." The Prime Minister glared at his watch. "Dear me, it's far too late for conditions. You'll just have to solve the problem yourself. I must hurry home and change my trousers."

He bent down to pick up his bat. "You a married man?" he enquired, glancing up at the Park Keeper.

"No, my lord, my Prime – er, no."

"Neither am I. A pity, that. Not from my own point of view, of course. But to think that there's someone dreaming of me – putting a bunch of herbs under her pillow – Lad's

Love, Lavender, Creeping Jenny – and then not finding me, poor woman. Alas, alas, what a disappointment! Tonight of all nights – you understand."

And he strode off, swinging his bat and his rose, his white trousers riding up from his ankles as though they had shrunk in the wash.

The Park Keeper did *not* understand. Who would be disappointed, and why? What was so special about tonight – except the fact that everyone seemed to be breaking the Bye-laws; using the Public Park as though it were their own back yard? And who could that be, he asked himself, as a curious figure, walking backwards, feet uncertainly feeling their way, came staggering through the Lane Gate?

It was Ellen from Number Seventeen, Cherry Tree Lane, moving like a sleep-walker, eyes closed, arms outstretched before her, meandering over the newly turfed lawn that he had mown this morning.

The Park Keeper braced himself. He would not stand meekly by while the Rules were not only not being Observed but illegally flouted. Come what might, this was something he would have to deal with, even without a hat. His eyes fell on a small object lying limply beside the fountain. It was the Prime Minister's cricketing cap, left behind, apparently, when he hurried off to change his trousers. The Park Keeper seized it gratefully. At least his head would be covered.

"Look where you're going! Be careful, Miss Ellen! Beware of swings and see-saws and such. Steer clear of benches, borders and baskets." He strode towards her shouting his warnings.

Slowly, carefully, sometimes sneezing, Ellen came backing in his direction. Then, just as she was almost upon him, the Policeman, suddenly spying her, neatly inserted himself between them and Ellen landed with a bump against his blue serge jacket.

"Oh!" she cried joyfully, as she turned about and opened her eyes. "I hoped it might be you – and it is! What if I had made a mistake and bumped into the wrong one!"

"What, indeed!" The Policeman beamed. "But you didn't. And I'm the right one, see, and no mistake about it."

"It *is* a mistake to do things like that. You might have knocked someone over or got yourself a broken leg. And then who'd be to blame? Me! No Backing allowed in a Public Park!" the Park Keeper warned her sternly.

"But I have to. It's Midsummer's Eve – atishoo! And if you walk backwards on Midsummer's Eve, after putting a herb or two under your pillow – Marjoram, Sweet Basil, no matter what – you'll back into your own true love as sure as nuts are nuts. Unless it's a gooseberry bush – atishoo! If it is, you have to wait till next year. To try again, I mean."

"Well, I'm no gooseberry bush, am I?" The Policeman took her hand in his. "So you won't have to wait till next year, will you?" He tucked his arm through hers.

"But what if you *never* bump into someone? What if it's *always* a gooseberry bush?" the Park Keeper demanded. It might be an Old Wives' Tale she was telling. But with these, he knew, you had to be careful. Unwise to make a mock of them: they were apt to turn out to be true.

"Oh, it's got to be someone someday – atishoo! There aren't all that many gooseberry bushes. And then there's the cucumber, don't forget!"

"What cucumber?" Was this some further silliness? Were they trying to make a fool of him?

"You don't know *anything*, do you?" said Ellen. "Didn't your Grandmother tell you nothing? Mine told it to me and hers told her. And *her* Grandmother told it to her, and away and away, right back to Adam."

He had been right, the Park Keeper thought. It *was* an Old Wives' Tale!

"Well, this is what you do," said Ellen. "You rub the juice behind your ears, close your eyes, put out your arms and then start walking backwards. It might be a long time or a short. Atishoo!" She paused to blow her nose. "But at last, if you're lucky, you meet your True Love."

She gave the Policeman a blushing glance. "It's witchy," she added, "very witchy. But – you'll see! – it's worth it."

"Nothing like cucumber!" the Policeman grinned. "Luckiest vegetable in the world! Well, you've met yours and I've met mine. So the next thing is to name the day. How about next Thursday?"

He took Ellen firmly by the hand and led her away across the grass, tossing aside, as he did so, a spill of toffee paper.

The Park Keeper sighed as he picked it up and gazed after the lovers.

What was to be his lot, he wondered. The world went strolling past in pairs, two by two, hand in hand. Would such a thing ever happen to him? Had herbs been tucked under someone's pillow in the hope of meeting Frederick Smith, the Park Keeper? Would anyone – Snow White, say, or Cinderella – hide her face in *his* serge jacket?

The sun had now laggardly slipped away, leaving behind the long blue twilight – not day, not night, but something in between – the hour that is thronged with fate.

The Prime Minister had disappeared and was even now, very likely, taking his top hat out of its hat box. Everyone else, apparently, was bent on their own affairs, even if those very affairs were ruining the Park. No one, as far as the Park Keeper could see, was looking in his direction.

What if – it was nonsense, of course – but what if he gave the thing a try? It certainly wouldn't do any harm. And it might, oh it might—! He crossed his fingers.

Straightening his blue flannel cap, the Park Keeper glanced furtively round, slipped a hand into his pocket and brought out the crumbling remains of his lunch – a scrap of cucumber sandwich. Cautiously, stealthily, he rubbed the scrap behind each ear and felt the juice of the cucumber as it trickled down into his collar. He summoned up his determination and drew a long, deep breath.

"Good luck, Fred!" he said to himself. Then he closed his eyes, stretched out his arms in front of him and began to walk slowly backwards. Easy now! Step by step. He gave himself to the twilight.

He seemed to be in another world. The Park he knew had dissolved itself into the darkness behind his eyes. Voices that had been near and lively grew faint and faded away. Distant music was wafted to him by people singing in chorus – old songs he seemed to have known as a boy, dreamy, gentle as lullabies. And somewhere a hurdy-gurdy was playing. Bert, the Match Man, of course!

Tch, tch! NO MUSICIANS OR HAWKERS ALLOWED IN THE PARK! But now the Bye-laws would have to wait. He had something else to do. From the right – or was it the left of him? – came the sound of splashing water. Oh, why wouldn't people look at the notice? NO SWIMMING PERMITTED IN THE LAKE. But perhaps it was just the fish rising, which was what they did at this hour of the day. You couldn't really blame them for that. Fish, after all, can't read.

On, on. His feet felt the bending grass beneath them and the spreading roots of trees. The scent of dandelions rose to his nose, something like dandelions brushed his boots. Where was he? In the Wild Garden? He could not tell and dared not look. If he opened his eyes, he might break the spell. On, on. Backwards, backwards. His destiny was leading him.

And now about him were whispering voices, rustlings and stirrings and stifled laughter.

"Hurry, you boys!" urged a man's deep voice that seemed to come from far above him. "We haven't got much time!"

Good Heavens, thought the Park Keeper. Were people actually up in the trees, breaking the branches as well as the Bye-laws? Never mind. He had to go on.

"We're coming!" piping voices answered, from the height of the Park Keeper's shoulder. "It's the others who are lagging behind. Come *on*, Foxy! And you too, Bear! Why must you always be such a slowcoach?"

Foxes? Bears? The Park Keeper trembled. Could it be that the Keeper of the Zoological Gardens, bewitched by this thing called Midsummer's Eve, had left the cages open? Might he himself, at any moment, be confronted with a jungle beast, a tiger burning bright?

"Oh, help!" he cried, leaping aside, as a furry form brushed his ankle. Not a tiger, he thought, too small and fleecy. A rabbit, it must be, a wild rabbit. No rabbits allowed in the Public Parks. He would set a trap tomorrow.

There were scurryings now all about him and a sudden swoop and clap of wings as an airy shape flew past.

Something that felt like a cherry-stone rapped on his cap and bounced away. It was as though it had been spat out by someone much taller than himself, imagining him – the Park Keeper – to be a Litter-basket. He was humming, this someone, as he strode by, a refrain that sounded familiar. Could it, perhaps, be *Pop Goes the Weasel*? If so, it was out of tune.

The humming died away behind him. All was silent. The world was still, his footsteps the only thing that moved.

The Park Keeper felt lost and lonely. His outstretched arms were beginning to ache. His eyes were weary of seeing nothing.

Even so, back and back he went. All things come to an end, he knew. And he would not fail whoever it was who was dreaming her Midsummer dream.

Blindly stumbling, backwards, backwards. And, after hours, it seemed, and miles – was he even still in the Park? – he heard about him a distant murmur: nothing festive, no great clamour, merely the friendly, sociable chatter of people at one with each other.

The murmur grew louder as he neared it. Somebody laughed. Voices were raised and then lowered. Conversation went back and forth. How beautiful, the Park Keeper thought, was the sound of human gossip! Whoever these people were, he was sure, the longed-for "she" would be among them. At last, at last, his fate was upon him. The time had come when he, Fred Smith, like everybody else in the world, would go hand in hand, two by two.

Nearer and nearer came the voices. How many more backward steps were needed? Three would do it, the Park Keeper thought. He took them slowly. One. Two. Three.

And suddenly – bump! There she was! His spine sensed the shape of a curving shoulder, slender and warm, and his heart leapt. All he need do now was turn and face her. He swivelled round upon his heel and a firm hand thrust him sideways.

"I'll thank you not to behave like a carthorse. I am not a lamp-post!" said Mary Poppins.

The voice was only too well known and the Park Keeper, still with his eyes closed, let out a cry of protest.

"Never no luck for me," he wailed. "I might have known it wouldn't work. Here I come, looking for my True Love, and I have to bump into a gooseberry bush!"

A cackle of laughter rent the air. "Some gooseberry bush!" jeered another voice he would rather not have heard.

With a groan, the Park Keeper opened his eyes and, as

though unwilling to believe what they told him, hurriedly closed them again.

He was in the Herb Garden, he realised, with its marble seats and its paved path round a square of chamomile lawn. There was nothing new in that, of course. He had planned and planted it himself. But now on the sward he had mown so often, among the remains of a recent picnic – egg-shells, cake, sausage rolls – were Mary Poppins and the Banks children, Mrs Corry and her two daughters, and his own mother sitting on one of the seats, smiling her welcoming smile.

Nothing new in all that either. But had he seen – yes, he had indeed – he could not deny his own eyes – a Bear sitting snugly beside the hedge, licking a trumpet of Honeysuckle; a Fox on its hind legs picking the Foxgloves; and a Hare in the Parsley patch!

And as if all this were not enough, Jane and Michael, wearing wreaths of green, together with two unknown boys, scantily clad and similarly crowned, were plucking armfuls of herbs; a big man, armed with a club and dressed in strips of leather, a studded belt about his waist and a lion-skin round his shoulders, was decking Mary Poppins' ear with a double stem of cherries; and a large bird, perched on a bough above her – this to him was the last straw! – was being regaled by the Bird Woman with a sprig of flowering Fennel!

"Mother, how *could* you?" the Park Keeper cried. "No Picking of Herbs allowed in the Park. You know the Bye-laws and you break them!"

This was the first time she had failed him and he felt he could never forgive her.

"Well, you got to make allowances, lad. He only comes down once a year."

"I'm not *allowed* allowances, Mum! And birds are coming down all the time. They can't make nests up there in the sky. After all, it stands to reason."

"Nothing stands to reason, Fred – not tonight, it doesn't." She glanced from the bird to the animals.

"Well, isn't it very reasonable to come and get the things you need? *I* would!" said Michael stoutly.

"But how did they get here to get what they need? Somebody let them out of the Zoo!" The cages *had* been unlocked! The Park Keeper was sure of it.

"No, no. They came down with Castor and Pollux." Jane waved her hand at the two boys, as she plucked a spray of Soloman's Seal and tucked it into her looped-up skirt.

"Castor and Pollux! Get along! They're characters in a story. Lily-white boys turned into stars. Tamed horses, that's what they did. I read it when I was a boy."

"And we came down with Orion," said the boys, speaking as though with a single voice. "We came to get fresh herbs for our horse, and he to pick cherries in the Lane. He always does on Midsummer's Eve."

"Oh, does he indeed?" The Park Keeper smiled a withering smile. "Just descends, like, out of the sky, to steal what belongs to the County Council! What do you take me for, then – an April Fool in the middle of June? Orion's up there, like he always is." He flung up a pointing finger.

"Where?" demanded the big man. "Show me!"

The Park Keeper craned his head backwards, but all he could see was emptiness, a large, vacant, unanswering sky, blue as the bloom on a plum.

"Well, you'll have to wait. It's not dark enough yet. But he'll be there, don't you worry – up there where he belongs."

Mrs Corry let out a cackle of laughter. "Who's worrying?" she shrieked.

"You're right," said the big man with a sigh, as he sat down on a marble seat and laid his club beside him. "Orion will be where he belongs. He can't do otherwise, poor chap." He took a cherry from the hoard in his hand, ate it and spat out the stone. "But not yet – ah, no, not yet. There's still a little time."

"Well, you'd better get off where *you* belong – a circus tent, I wouldn't wonder, with all that fol de rol fancy dress. *And* you!" the Park Keeper waved at the boys. "Tight-rope walkers or I'm a Dutchman!"

"You're a Dutchman then! We're Gallopers!" The boys burst into a peal of laughter.

"One thing or the other, it makes no difference. Leave the leaves and I'll burn them tomorrow. We don't want no ragamuffins here."

"They're not ragamuffins! Oh, can't you see?" Jane was almost in tears.

"But what will Pegasus do?" cried Michael, angrily stamping his foot. "They wanted a meal of Coltsfoot for him. So I gathered it. I don't *want* it burnt!" He hugged the herb-filling string bag to him, determined to defy the Bye-laws.

"Pegasus!" scoffed the Park Keeper. "He's another of them taradiddles. You learn about them when you're at school. *Astronomy for Boys and Girls.* Constellations, comets and such. But whoever saw a horse with wings? He's just a bunch of stars, that's all. And Vulpecula, and Ursa Minor and Lepus – all that lot."

"What important names." The two boys giggled. "We call them Foxy and Bear and Hare."

"Call them anything you like. Just get out of here, the three of you. And take your circus beasts along or I'll go to the Zoo and find the Keeper and have them put behind bars."

"If a gooseberry bush may make a remark?" Mary Poppins broke in. "You did say gooseberry bush, I believe?" she said with icy politeness.

The Park Keeper quailed before her glance.

"It was just a-a kind of manner of speaking. And gooseberry bush is no libel, it's just a sort of – er – spiky shrub. And anyway, put it in a nutshell –" Why shouldn't he speak his mind, he thought. "It isn't as though you're the Queen of Sheba."

The big man sprang from the marble seat.

"Who says she's not?" he demanded sternly, and the lion-skin stiffened on his shoulder, the head showing its fangs.

The Park Keeper hurriedly took a step backwards.

"Well, no one can say she is, can they? What with turned-up nose and turned-out feet and a knob of hair and—"

"What's wrong with them?" The big man glowered,

reaching for the club at his side and looming over the Park Keeper, who hurriedly took another step backwards.

Majestically, a pink and white statue, Mary Poppins inserted herself between them. "If you're looking for the Keeper of the Zoological Gardens, he is not in the Zoo. He is in the Lake."

"In the *Lake*?" The Park Keeper stared at her aghast. "D-drownded?" he whispered, pale as a lily. Oh, alas, alas!"

"Paddling. With the Lord Mayor and two Aldermen. Fishing for tiddlers to put in a jam-jar."

"J-jam-jar? The Lord Mayor? Oh, no! Oh, no! Not tiddlers. It's against the B-bye-laws. Isn't *anyone* Observing the Rules?" the Park Keeper cried in despair.

The world, as he knew it, had fallen apart. Where now was the lawful authority that he had always served? To whom could he turn for reassurance? The Policeman? No, he was off with Ellen. The Lord Mayor – oh, horrors! – was in the Lake. The Prime Minister was closeted with the King. And he himself, the Park's Park Keeper, important though he undoubtedly was, must carry the burden alone.

"Why should it all depend on me?" He flung his arms wide with the question. "All right, I took off a bit of time, which is owed me, after all. And it wasn't much to ask," he lamented. "Only to find my own True Love —"

"Curly Locks, I suppose, or Rapunzel?" Mrs Corry chuckled. "You'll find they're suited, I'm afraid. But I've got a couple of soncy girls – Fannie and Annie, take your pick – and I'll throw in a pound of tea!"

The Park Keeper put the suggestion aside as being beneath his notice.

"To find my True Love," he repeated. "And all Litter placed in the proper baskets. No Stealing of Herbs from here, nor Cherries from the Lane. No one pretending to be what they're not." He waved at the intruders. "And everyone keeping the Bye-laws."

"If you ask me, that's a lot to ask." The big man looked at him sternly. "True Loves don't grow on trees, you know."

"Or gooseberry bushes," Mary Poppins put in.

"And what are cherries for but eating? Herbs too, if it comes to that." The big man swallowed another cherry, and spat out another stone.

"But you can't just pick them because you want them!" The Park Keeper was scandalised.

"Why else?" enquired the big man mildly. "If we didn't want them, we wouldn't take them."

"Because you've got to think of others." The Park Keeper, who seldom thought of others himself, was quick to deliver his sermon. "That's why we have the Bye-laws, see!"

"Well, we *are* the others, all of us. And so are you, my man."

"Me!" The Park Keeper was indignant. "I'm not somebody else, not me!"

"Of course you are. Everyone's somebody else to someone. And what harm have the wild beasts done? A few green leaves one day in the year! It's true that they're not used to Bye-laws. We don't have them up there, thank goodness." The big man nodded at the sky.

"And as for pretending to be what we're not – or what you presume to think we're not – how about yourself? Making all this fuss and pother, meddling in things that don't concern you – isn't it rather presumptuous? You're behaving as though you owned the place. Why not look after your own affairs and leave the Park to the Park Keeper? He seems a sensible sort of chap. I always enjoy looking down at him – mowing the lawns, putting waste paper into containers, faithfully going about his job."

The Park Keeper stared.

"But it's *my* job he's going about. I mean that *I'm* going about it. Don't you see? He's me!"

"Who's you?"

"Him. I mean me. *I'm* the Park Keeper."

"Nonsense! I've seen him often enough. A decent young fellow, neat and natty. Wears a peaked cap with PK on it, not a silly little blue flannel top-knot."

The Park Keeper clapped his hand to his head. The Prime Minister's cap! He had quite forgotten. Perhaps he should never have worn it.

"Look here," he said, with the fearful calm of one who is near his wits' end. "I'm the same man, aren't I, whatever my cap?" Surely it was obvious. Had circus people no brains at all?

"Well, *are* you? Only you can give an answer to that. And it's not an easy question. I wonder..." The big man was suddenly thoughtful. "I wonder, would I be the same person without my belt and lion-skin?"

"*And* your club. *And* your faithful dog-star. Don't forget Sirius, Orion!" The two boys laughed and teased him. "Sirius can't come down with us," they explained to Jane and Michael. "He'd be chasing all the cats in the Lane."

"Yes, yes, the fellow has a point. Even so," the big man went on, "I can't believe the Keeper I know, that watchful, conscientious servant, would go walking backwards through the Park, eyes closed, hands outstretched, and bits of crust behind his ears. And on top of that – without a 'By your leave' or 'I beg your pardon' – go bumping into an elegant lady as though she were a lamp-post."

The Park Keeper put his hands to his ears. It was true. They were decked with scraps of sandwich!

"Well," he blustered, "how was I to know she was there? And it wasn't the bread that was important. What I wanted was cucumber."

"A proper Park Keeper doesn't go about bumping. And he knows how to get just what he wants. If cucumber, then why bread? You should be more precise."

"I know what *I* want," said a voice from the hedge. "A little of something sweet."

"Have a finger!" Mrs Corry shrieked, as she broke off one from her left hand and offered it to the Bear. "Don't worry, it will grow again!"

His small eyes widened with surprise. "Barley sugar!" he exclaimed with delight, and stuffed it into his mouth.

"Nothing for nothing!" said Mrs Corry. "Put a shine on my coat for luck!"

The Bear put his paw upon her collar. "It'll shine, when it's time – just wait!" he said.

"What I want is a pair of gloves. I'm going to a party tonight and I like to look well-dressed." The Fox prinked and pranced beside the Foxgloves, as he tried on flower after flower.

"Parsley!" said the Hare from the Parsley patch.

"For his rheumatism," the big man explained. "It's often cold up there and draughty. And Parsley's good for it."

"Coo-roo, coo-roo," the great Bird crooned as he munched his Fennel.

> "*I do*
> *Like a herb*
> *Or two,*
> *Don't you?*"

The Park Keeper's eyes, as large as soup plates, swivelled in all directions.

Had he seen? Had he heard? A finger turned into Barley Sugar? Animals speaking in human voices? No, of course he hadn't! Yes, he had! Was it a dream? Had he gone mad?

"It's the cucumber!" he cried wildly. "I shouldn't have done it. Not behind the ears. She said it would be witchy. And it is! But whether it's worth it, I'm not sure. Maybe I'm not the Park Keeper. Maybe I *am* somebody else. Everything's head over heels tonight. I don't know nothing, not any more."

And snatching the cricket cap from his head, he flung himself, sobbing, across the lawn and buried his face in his mother's skirt.

She smoothed his ruffled hair with her hand. "Don't take on so vainly, Fred. It'll come right – you'll see."

The big man regarded him broodingly.

"A sprig of Heartsease or Lemon balm – either of them would be soothing. Probably needs a rest from himself, whoever he is, poor chap! I even get tired of being Orion." He sighed and shook his head.

"*We* don't need a rest from ourselves, do we?" Castor and Pollux exchanged a grin.

"Ah, that's because you've got each other. But it's often lonely, away up there."

"I never get tired of being myself. I like being Michael Banks," said Michael. "And so does Mary Poppins. I mean, she likes being Mary Poppins. Don't you, Mary Poppins?"

"Who else would I want to be, pray?" She gave him one of her haughty looks. The very idea was absurd.

"Ah, well, but you're the Great Exception. We can't all be like you, can we?" Orion gave her a sidelong glance and picked out another pair of cherries. "That's for your other ear, my dear."

"I've no complaints," the Bear bumbled. "I like showing sailors the way home."

"I'm going to be a sailor," said Michael. "Aunt Flossie sent me this suit for my birthday."

"Well, you'll need the star in my tail to guide you. I am always there."

"Not if I have Mary Poppins' compass. I can go right round the world with that. And she can stay here and look after my children."

"Thank you, Michael Banks, I'm sure. If I've nothing better to do than that," she gave a loud, affronted sniff, "I'll be sorry for myself."

"Come to the party, that's something better – me in my beautiful foxgloves and you in your new pink dress." The Fox danced on his hind legs and held up his foxgloved paws. "The handsome Mr Vulpecula, arm in arm with Miss Mary Poppins!"

"Handsome is as handsome does." Mary Poppins, with a toss of her head, tossed aside the invitation.

"There's poison in Foxgloves," said Michael glibly. "Mary Poppins never let us wear them in case we happen to lick our fingers and then have to go to bed, and be sick."

"Foxes do not lick their paws, nothing so vulgar," said the Fox. "They merely wash them in the evening dew."

"Parsley," said a voice from the Parsley patch, with a coughing, choking sound.

Orion sprang from his marble seat.

"Be careful, Lepus, don't eat it! Spit it out, whatever it is! Ah, that's better. There's a good Hare!" He fossicked among the curling fronds and held up a shiny circular object. "A half-crown piece, by all that's lucky! And he nearly swallowed it."

The four children clustered about it, gazing greedily at the coin.

"What will you spend it on?" Jane asked.

"How could I spend it? There's nothing to buy. There are no ice cream carts in the sky, no peppermint horses, no balloons, not even…" he glanced at Mrs Corry, "not even a gingerbread star."

"Well, what *is* up there? Nothing but nothing?" Michael found that hard to believe.

"Just space." Orion shrugged his shoulders. "Though you can't exactly say space is nothing."

"And there's lots of room," said Castor and Pollux. "Pegasus gallops everywhere and we take it in turns to ride him."

Michael felt a twinge of envy. He wished he could ride a horse through the sky.

"Room? Who wants room?" Orion grumbled. "Down here you have no room at all. Everything's close to something else. Houses leaning against each other. Trees and bushes crowding together. Pennies and half-pennies clinking in pockets. Friends and neighbours always at hand. Someone to talk to, someone to listen. Ah, well," he sighed, "each to his fate."

He tossed the silver coin in the air.

"Tails up, and you two can have it." He nodded at Jane and Michael. "Heads, and I keep it myself."

Down came the coin on his outstretched palm. "Heads it is. Hooray!" he cried. "If I can't spend it, at least I can wear it. I like a bit of bric-a-brac."

He pressed the half-crown against his belt in line with the three studs already there. "How does it look? Too flimsy? Too vulgar?"

"Oh, it's lovely!" all four children exclaimed.

"Neat enough," said Mary Poppins. "You'll need to keep it polished."

"Gingerbreadish, I'd say," giggled Mrs Corry. "A souvenir to remember us by."

"Souvenir!" Orion growled. "As if I needed reminding."

"He's right. He doesn't," said Castor and Pollux. "He pines all the year for Midsummer's Eve – this is our one night of magic – and the Park and the cherries and the music."

"Don't you have music up there?" asked Jane.

"Well," said Orion, "the morning stars sing together, of course. Same old plainsong day in and day out. But none of your cheerful, homely things. *Polly Wolly Doodle, Skip to my Lou, Pop Goes the What-you-call-it* – all that stuff. Listen! They're singing down by the Lake. Don't tell me, I'll get it in a minute. Ah, yes – *Green Grow the Rushes-O*." He hummed a line of the song.

"He can't sing in tune," the two boys whispered. "But he doesn't know it and we don't tell him."

"And then there's the music of the spheres, a sort of steady, droning sound. Rather like that spinning thing I saw you with today."

"My humming top! I'll get it," said Jane.

She ran to the perambulator that was like an over-crowded bird's nest, with John and Barbara and Annabel asleep on each other's shoulders.

Jane thrust in her hand and rummaged among them.

"It's not here. Oh, I've lost my top!"

"No, you haven't," said a gloomy voice, as a thin man and a fat woman came hand in hand into the Garden. "It fell out on to the Long Walk and we found it as we came by."

"It's Mr and Mrs Turvy!" cried Michael, as he dashed away to greet them.

"Well, it may be and it may not. You can't be certain of anything. Not today, you can't. You think you're this and you find you're that. You want to hurry, so you crawl like a snail." The thin man gave a doleful sigh.

"Oh, Cousin Arthur," Mary Poppins protested. "It's not your Second Monday, not one of your upside-down days!"

"I'm afraid it is, Mary, my dear. And tonight of all nights, when I want to go looking for my own True Love, just like everyone else."

"But you've already found her, Arthur!" Mrs Turvy reminded him.

"So you say, Topsy. And I'd like to believe it. But nothing's sure on the Second Monday."

"You'll be sure tomorrow. Tomorrow's Tuesday."

"And what if tomorrow never comes? It would be just like it to stay away." Mr Turvy was unconvinced. "Well, here's your top and much good may it do you." He turned aside, wiping an eye, as Jane set the coloured top on the path.

"Not yet, not yet!" Orion cried, suddenly cupping his hand to his ear.

From somewhere among the surrounding trees a bird gave a quick enquiring chirp that was followed by a rush of half-notes, not so much song as a series of kisses.

"A nightingale tuning up. Oh, glory!" Orion's face was alight with joy.

"It belongs to Mr Twigley," said Michael. "It's the only one in the Park."

"Some people do have all the luck. To own a nightingale! Think of it! Come on, come on, my lovely boy! Spin your old humming top, Jane! He'll outsing it, be sure."

The four children fell on the shining toy, shouldering each other aside, arguing and complaining.

"I'll start it! No, you won't, it's mine! Me! Me! Me!" they all shouted.

"Is this a Herb Garden or a Bear Pit?" demanded Mary Poppins.

"Certainly not a Bear Pit. Bears are better behaved," said the Bear.

"But, Mary Poppins, it's not fair!" Castor and Pollux protested. "We haven't got a top up there. They might give us a chance."

"Well, we haven't got a flying horse!" Jane and Michael were equally indignant.

Mary Poppins folded her arms and favoured them all with her fierce blue glance.

"Hooligans, the lot of you!" she said. "You haven't got this and you haven't got that. Tops or horses – take what you're given. Nobody has everything."

And in spite, or perhaps because of her fierceness that embraced them all equally, their anger melted away.

Castor and Pollux sat back on their heels. "Not even you, Mary Poppins?" they teased her. "With your new pink dress and your daisy hat?"

"And your carpet bag! And your parrot umbrella!" Jane and Michael joined in.

She preened a little at the compliment as she gave her characteristic sniff. "That's as may be," she retorted. "And no affair of yours either. I will start the top myself!"

She stooped to seize the handle, and pumped it briskly up and down.

Slowly, the top began to turn and as it turned, it hummed – faintly at first but gradually, as it gathered speed, the sound became one long deep note, filling the Herb Garden with its music, a bee-like humming and drumming.

"A ring! Make a ring!" cried Castor and Pollux. "The Grand Chain, everyone!"

And at once they all came into a circle, formally moving round the top as the earth moves round the sun. Right hand to right hand, left hand to left – the Bear with his sugar-stick in his mouth, the Fox dapper in his Foxgloves, the Hare nib-nibbling a sprig of Parsley.

Round and round. Hand to hand. Mary Poppins and the two Banks children, Mrs Corry, her daughters and the Bird Woman, Mr Turvy dragging his feet, Mrs Turvy dancing.

Round and round. Hand to hand. Orion girt with his lion-skin, Pollux with his tunic full of herbs, and Michael's string bag, bursting with Coltsfoot, slung about Castor's neck.

Round and round, each hand taking the hand of each, and the big Bird flying among them. The top spun and the circle spun round it, and the Park round the circle, the earth round the Park and the darkening sky round the earth.

The Nightingale, now the night was come, came to the full of his song. *Jug, jug, jug, tereu!* it went, over and over, from the elder tree, outsinging the hum of the top. The song would never be done, it seemed, and the top would never stop spinning. The circle of humans and constellations would go on turning for ever.

But suddenly the bird was silent and the top, with a last musical cry, slowed down and toppled sideways.

Clang! The tin shape crashed upon the flagstones.

And the Park Keeper sat up with a start.

He rubbed his eyes as though waking from sleep. Where was he? What had been happening? He had hidden himself from the fading day and all its unbearable problems. And now the day had disappeared. It had passed through its long blue twilight hour and had almost become the night.

But that was not all. The Herb Garden he knew so well was now another garden. There, in a ring, were people he knew, the familiar solid and substantial shapes of Mary Poppins and her charges, Mrs Corry and her two large daughters, his Mother in her shabby shawl. But who were the others, the bevy of transparent figures, the creatures that seemed to be made of light – insubstantial luminous boys hand in hand with substantial children; a man in a lion-skin, bright as the sun, bending towards Mary Poppins; a Bear and a Hare, both shimmering, a big Bird lifting wings of light and a sparkling Fox with flowers on his paws?

And suddenly, like a man who has lost, and regained, his senses, the Park Keeper understood. He had known those figures when he was a boy, and many more besides. And he had forgotten what he had known, denied it, made it a thing of naught, something to be sneered at! He put his hands up to his eyes to hide the springing tears.

Mary Poppins stooped and picked up the top.

"It's time," she said quietly. "The day is gone. You are needed now elsewhere. Castor, put your wreath on straight. And you, Pollux, fasten your collar. Remember who you are!"

"And who *you* are, Mary Poppins!" they teased her. "With your 'spit-spot and away you go!' As if we could ever forget!" They gathered their loads of greenstuff to them.

"Till next year, Jane and Michael," they cried. "We'll be coming to get more Coltsfoot!"

They flung up shining hands as they spoke and then, like the day, they were gone.

"And another pair of gloves!" said the Fox.

"More Barley Sugar!" the Bear bumbled.

"Parsley!" The one word came from the Hare.

And they too disappeared.

"*Coo-roo-coo-roo,*
This is for you!"

The great Bird swooped to Mary Poppins, stuck a wing feather into her hat and then became air and starlight.

Mary Poppins straightened the glowing feather and glanced up at Orion.

"Do not linger!" she warned him.

> *"Linger longer, Lucy,*
> *Linger longer, Lou,*
> *How I long to linger longer,*
> *To linger longa you."*

Orion sang tunelessly, and gave her a rueful glance.

"Don't worry, I'll be where I belong, just as that fellow said. "But – to leave all this –" He flung out his arms, as if to embrace the whole width of the Park. "Oh, well – the Law's the Law! But it's no easy thing to obey it." He gobbled up his remaining cherries, spat out the stones on the chamomile lawn, and took her hand and kissed it.

"Fare thee well, my fairy fay," he said gruffly. And then, like a candle flame blown out, he was there no longer.

"Next year!" cried Jane and Michael shrilly, to the emptiness he had left.

And at that the Park Keeper leapt to his feet.

"No, *now!*" he cried. "They can have them now – all they want, and more."

In a frenzy he dashed from bed to bed, plucking green branches of every kind and tossing them into the air.

"Take them! I'll let the Bye-laws be! Rosemary for Remembrance, mister. All the fodder you need, lads, for the horse! Foxgloves for the Foxy! Sweet savours for the beasts and the Bird."

He flung the herbs wildly towards the sky. And to the surprise of Jane and Michael, not a leaf, not a branch, came down – except a small spray of something that Mary Poppins caught in her hand and tucked into her belt.

"Forgive me, friends! I didn't reckernise you!" the Park Keeper called to the nothingness. "And I didn't reckernise meself, neither. I forgot what I knew when I was a boy. It needed the dark to show things plain. But I know who you are now, all of you. And I know who I am, Orion, sir! Cucumber or no cucumber, I'm the Park Keeper with or without my hat!"

And off he darted among the herbs, gathering, bellowing their names, tossing them into the air.

"St John's Wort! Marigold! Coriander! Cornflower! Dandelion! Marjoram! Rue!"

"Really, Smith, you should be more careful! You might have knocked my eye out."

Mr Banks, entering the Herb Garden, removed a sprig of Marjoram from the brim of his bowler hat. "And of course you are the Park Keeper! Whoever said you weren't?"

The Park Keeper took no notice. On he went, madly tossing and yelling. "Good King Henry! Rampion! Sage! Sweet Cicely! Rocket! Basil!"

Up into the air went leaves and flowers and none of them came down.

Mr Banks stared after him.

"What's he doing, throwing herbs around? A Park Keeper breaking the Bye-laws! The poor chap must have lost his wits."

"Or found them!" said the Bird Woman softly.

"Aha! So this is where you are!" Mr Banks turned and raised his hat. "I missed you as I came by St Paul's. Your birds were making an awful to-do. Don't they ever stop eating? And no one was there to take my tuppence, so now, of course, they're starving. Well, what are all of you doing here?"

He held out his arms to the children. "A Midsummer picnic, I presume. You might have left me a sausage roll." He picked up a discarded piece of pastry and munched it hungrily.

"Are you looking for your own True Love?" Jane asked, hugging him.

"Of course not. I know where she is. I'm on my way to her now, as it happens. And how are *you*, Mary Poppins?" he asked, glancing at the upright figure as it rocked the perambulator. "You're looking very sprightly tonight, with a spray of forget-me-not in your belt and your cherry earrings and Sunday-best hat. That feather must have cost a pretty penny!"

"Thank you, I'm sure." She tossed her head, and smiled her self-satisfied smile. Compliments were no more than her due and she always accepted them calmly.

He gave her a thoughtful, puzzled glance. "You never get older, Mary Poppins, do you? What's the secret? Tell me!" he teased her.

"Ah, that's because she's eaten Fern seed!" The Bird Woman eyed him slyly.

"Fern seed? Nonsense! An Old Wives' Tale. 'Eat Fern seed and you'll live for ever', they told me when I was a boy. And I used to come and look for it, here in this very garden."

"I can't imagine you as a boy." Jane measured her height against his waistcoat button.

"I don't see why not." Mr Banks was hurt. "I was a very charming boy – about as high as you are now – in brown velveteen and a white collar and black stocking and button-up boots. 'Fern seed, fern seed, where are you?' I'd say. But of course I never found it. I'm not even sure that it exists." Mr Banks looked sceptical.

"And, what was worse, I lost something – the first half-crown I ever had. Oh, the dreams I dreamed of that half-crown. I was going to buy the world with it. But it must have dropped out of a hole in my pocket."

"That must be the one Orion found. He took it away with him," said Michael. "Just before you came."

"O'Ryan? A friend of Smith's, I suppose! Those Irish fellows have all the luck. He's probably spent it by now, the wretch! If I had turned up earlier, I'd have made him give it back. I can't afford to lose pennies, let alone half-crowns."

Mary Poppins regarded him sagely. "All that's lost is somewhere," she told him.

Mr Banks stared at her. For a moment he seemed quite mystified and then, of a sudden, his face cleared. He flung back his head and laughed.

"Of course! Why didn't I think of that? It couldn't fall out of the universe, could it? Everything has to be somewhere. Even so," he sighed, "it would have been useful. Well, no good crying over spilt milk. I must get on. I'm late already."

A hen-like screech rent the air. "You always were!" a voice cackled. "Late in the morning. Late at night. You'll be late for your funeral, if you don't look out!"

Mr Banks, startled, peered through the dusk and saw, half-hidden by the elder-tree, a little old woman in a black coat that was covered with – could it be? – threepenny bits! And beside her two large, formless shapes that might, or might not, be younger ladies.

It was true. He had to admit it. He *was* in the habit of not being on time. But how did this old person know it? And what right had she, a complete stranger, to meddle in his affairs?

"Well," he began defensively, "I'm a busy man, I'd have you know. Making money to keep my family; often working late at the office – it's hard to wake up in the morning—"

"Early to bed, early to rise, makes a man healthy and wealthy and wise. I said that to Ethelred the Unready. But, of course, he wouldn't listen."

"*Ethelred the Unready!*" Mr Banks was astonished. "But he was around ten hundred and something!" She's dotty, poor thing, he thought to himself, I must humour her. "And what about Alfred the Great?" he asked. "Was he a friend of yours too?"

"Ha! He was worse than Ethelred. Promised to watch my cakes, he did. 'No need to move them' I said to him. 'Just keep the fire going – and watch!' And what did he do? Piled up the logs and then forgot. Just sat there, brooding over his kingdom, while my gingerbread stars were cooked to a crisp."

"*Gingerbread stars!*" Whatever next? Really, Mr Banks told himself, Mary Poppins certainly had a gift for making peculiar friends!

"Well, never mind," he said soothingly. "You've still got the real stars, haven't you? They can't get cooked or move from their places."

He ignored her scream of mocking laughter as he glanced up at the sky.

"Ah, there's the first one! Wish on it, children. And another! They're coming thick and fast. Good Lord, they are so bright tonight!" His voice was soft with rapture.

"Star light, star bright," he murmured. "It's as though they were having a party up there. Polaris! Sirius! The Heavenly Twins! And where is – ah, yes, there he is! I can always tell him by his belt with its three great stars in a row. Great Heavens!" He gave a start of surprise. "There are *four* in a row, or my eyesight's failing. Jane! Michael! Can you see it? An extra star beside the others?"

Their eyes followed his pointing finger. And, sure enough, faint and small, there was a something – not, perhaps, to be claimed as a star – and yet, and yet, a something!

They blinked at it, half-afraid to believe but, even so, half-believing.

"I *think* I see it," they both whispered. They did not dare to be sure.

Mr Banks threw his hat into the air. He was beside himself with joy.

"A new star! Clap your hands, world! And I, George Banks, of Number Seventeen, Cherry Tree Lane, have been the first to spot it. But let me be calm, yes, calm's the word – let me be cool, composed and placid."

But, far from being any of these, he was feverish with

excitement. "I must go at once to the Admiral and ask for the use of his telescope. Verify it. Tell the Astronomer Royal. You'll find your way, won't you, Mary Poppins? This is important, you understand. Goodnight, Mrs Smith!" He bowed to the Bird Woman. "And goodnight to you, madam – er – hum—"

"Corry," said Mrs Corry, grinning.

Mr Banks, already streaking away, stopped dead in his tracks.

When had he heard that name before? He stared at the oddity before him and turned, for some reason, to Mary Poppins.

The two women were regarding him gravely, silent and motionless as pictured figures in a book, looking out from the page.

Suddenly, Mr Banks was flooded with a sense of being somewhere else. And, also, of being someone else who was, at the same time, himself.

White-collared and velvet-suited, he was standing on tiptoe in button-up boots, his nose just reaching a glass-topped counter, over which he was handing to someone he could hardly see, a precious threepenny bit. The place smelt richly of gingerbread; an ancient woman was slyly asking, "What will you do with the gold paper?" and a voice that seemed to be his own was saying, "I keep them under my pillow."

"Sensible boy," the old creature croaked, exchanging a nod with someone behind him, someone wearing a straw hat with a flower or two springing from it.

"George, where are you?"

Another and younger voice cried his name. "George! George!"

And the spell was broken.

With a start, Mr Banks returned to the Herb Garden and all familiar things. It had been nothing, he told himself, a moment's madness, a slip of the mind.

"Impossible!" He laughed nervously, as he met Mary Poppins' glance.

"All things are possible," she said primly.

His eyebrows went up. Was she mocking him?

"Even the impossible?" he asked, mocking her in return.

"Even that," she assured him.

"George!" The calling voice held a note of panic.

"I'm here," he answered. "Safe and sound!" He turned away from the moonstruck moment, the trance, the dream, whatever it was.

"After all," he thought, "it's Midsummer's Eve. One expects to be bewitched."

"Oh, George," cried Mrs Banks, wringing her hands, "the children are off on a supper picnic. And I can't find them. I'm afraid they are lost!"

He strode towards the fluttering shape that was crossing the lawn towards him.

"How could they be lost? They're with Mary Poppins. We can trust her to bring them home. For you're coming with me, my True Love. Wonderful news! Guess what it is! I think I've discovered a new star and I want to look at it through a spyglass. If it's true, I'll be made Star-Gazer-in-Chief and you shall be Queen of the May."

"Don't be silly, George," she giggled. "You and your stars! You're always making fun of me." But she didn't mind him being silly and she liked being called his True Love.

"Admiral! Admiral! Wait for us! We want to look through your tel-es-co-pe!"

Mr Banks' voice, a fading echo, came floating back to the Herb Garden. And, at the same moment, the chorus of singers by the Lake came to the end of their song.

> "*Two, two are the lily-white boys,*
> *A-clothed all in green-o*
> *One is one and all alone*
> *And ever more shall be so!*"

"Ever more," the Bird Woman murmured, glancing up at the sky. "Well, I must be getting along. I've a dish of Irish stew on the hob and he'll be hungry when he gets home."

She nodded in the direction of the Park Keeper who was still tossing twigs and branches and crying their names to the air.

"Good King Henry! Mistletoe! Lovage! All you want, Sir and lads!"

And none of them came down.

"Come, Arthur," said Mrs Turvy. "It's time we were going home."

"If we *have* a home," grumbled Mr Turvy, still very

down in the dumps. "What about fires and earthquakes, Topsy? Anything could have happened."

"Nothing has happened to it – you'll see. Come to tea on Thursday, Mary. Things will be better then." Mrs Turvy led her husband away, guiding him through the shadows.

"Wait for me, Mrs Smith, my dear!" Mrs Corry gave her bird-like shriek. The threepenny bits on her coat were a-twinkle and the spot on her collar where the Bear had touched it now shone like a glowing button. "I have to get my beauty sleep or what will Prince Charming say – tee-hee?" She grinned at her two large daughters.

"Stir your stumps, Fannie and Annie," she said. "Come home and stuff some herbs under your pillows – Sowbread and Cuckoo's Meat might do the trick! – and perhaps I'll get you off my hands. Handsome husbands and ten thousand a year. Shake a leg, you galumphing giraffes! Pull up your socks! Skedaddle!"

She made a curtsey to Mary Poppins who received it with a gracious bow. Then away she went, prancing in her elastic boots between her plodding daughters, with the Bird Woman sailing along beside them, like a full-rigged ship, on the grass.

The Herb Garden, so lately full of light and movement, was still now, a pool of darkness.

"Jane, take your top," said Mary Poppins. "It is time we too were going home." And the many-coloured tin planet that hummed and spun so harmoniously was stowed away with the picnic things, silent and motionless, as Jane swung the basket from her hand.

Michael looked round for his string bag and suddenly remembered.

"I've nothing to carry, Mary Poppins," he complained.

"Carry yourself," she told him briskly, as she turned to the perambulator and gave it a vigorous push. "Step along, please, and best foot forward."

"Which is the best foot, Mary Poppins?"

"The one that's in front, of course!"

"But it's sometimes the left and sometimes the right. They can't both be the best," he protested.

"Michael Banks!" She gave him one of her savage looks. "If you are determined to argle-bargle, you can stay here and do it all by yourself. *We* are going home."

He did, indeed, want to argle-bargle and, if he could, get the better of her. But he knew that she always won in the end. And, anyway, it would be no fun to argue with the empty air since it could not answer back.

He decided he would carry himself. But how did one do that, he wondered. He could do it more easily, he thought, with something in his hand. So he seized on the handle of the perambulator and, to his surprise, became a boy who was carrying himself.

Jane came to the other side so that, with Mary Poppins between, all three were pushing together. They were suddenly glad to feel her nearness in the wide unfamiliar darkness.

For this was no longer their daytime Park, their intimate ordinary playground. They had never before been up so late nor understood that night changes the world and makes the known unknown. The trees that, by daylight, were merely trees – something to shade you from the sun or swing on when the Park Keeper was not looking – were now strange beings with a life of their own, full of secrets never disclosed, holding their breath till you went past.

Camellias, Rhododendrons, Lilacs, that by day were clustering shapes of green, were now nameless creatures full of menace, lying in wait, ready to spring.

The night itself was a whole new country, unmapped and unexplored, where the only thing that could not be doubted was the steady moving shape between them; flesh and bone under its cotton dress, the well-worn handbag and parrot umbrella aswing from the crook of its arm. They felt it rather than saw it, for they dared not lift their eyes. Nor could they be sure, in this crowding darkness, of the brightness they had seen. Or had they really seen it at all? Might they not have dreamed it?

To the right of them a bush moved. It muttered and mumbled to itself. Was it about to pounce?

They huddled closer to the cotton dress.

"It must be somewhere," the bush was saying. "I had to take it off, I remember, in order to find the letter."

With an effort the children lifted their heads and nervously peered through the dark. They had come, they saw, to the Rose Garden. And the bush, edging forward as if to spring, became, by magic, a man. Ceremoniously clad, in top hat, black jacket and striped trousers, he was crawling about on hands and knees, clearly looking for something.

"I've lost my cricket cap," he told them. "Here, by the fountain or under the roses. I don't suppose any of you have seen it?"

"It's in the Herb Garden," said Mary Poppins.

The Prime Minister sat back on his heels. "*In the Herb Garden!* But that's at the other end of the Park! However could it have got there? Cricket caps can't fly. Or maybe..." He glanced around uneasily. "Maybe they can on a night like this. Strange things happen, you know, on Midsummer's Eve." He scrambled to his feet.

"Well, I've just got time," he looked at his watch, "to fetch it and get to the Palace." He doffed his hat to Mary Poppins, stumbled away into the darkness and bumped into a clump of bushes that was stealthily moving towards him.

"Really!" The Prime Minister uttered the exclamation as he hurriedly jumped aside. "You shouldn't go creeping about like that – as though you were tracking tigers or something. It gave me quite a start."

"Hssssst!" hissed a bush. "Where's the Park Keeper?"

"My dear fellow, how should I know? I don't keep Park Keepers in my pocket. Nothing's in its right place tonight. He could be anywhere. Why do you want him?"

The clump shuffled a little nearer and became the Lord Mayor and two Aldermen. Their robes were looped up round their waists and their bare legs shone whitely in the dark.

"That's just it. I *don't* want him. We need to get safely out of the Park without him getting his eyes on these." The Lord

Mayor drew back a fold of his cloak and revealed a large glass jam-jar.

"Tiddlers! You'll catch it if he finds you. The Lord Mayor breaking his own Bye-laws! Ask that lady over there." The Prime Minister nodded at Mary Poppins. "She told me where to find my cap. And I must be off to get it. Goodnight!"

The Lord Mayor turned. "Why, it's you, Miss Poppins. How fortunate!" He glanced around warily and tiptoed over the grass.

"I wonder," he whispered into her ear, "if by any chance you've come across—"

"The Park Keeper?" Mary Poppins enquired.

"Sh! Not so loud. He might hear you."

"No, he won't." She favoured him with a Sphinx-like look. "He's far away at the end of the Park."

Gooseberry bush or no gooseberry bush, she was not going to disclose the fact that the Park Keeper, if only for tonight, was letting Bye-laws be.

"Splendid!" The Lord Mayor beckoned the Aldermen to him. "We can nip off home along the Lane and help ourselves…" he winked at them, "to a cherry or two as we go!"

"I think you will find they have all been picked," Mary Poppins informed them.

"What – *all*?" The three were scandalised. "Vandalism! We must speak to the King. What can the world be coming to?" They spoke to each other in outraged whispers as they scurried off with the jam-jar.

The perambulator creaked on its way. Tall, ghostly shapes

loomed up before it and turned into swings as it came nearer. A thick black shadow went past sneezing and then revealed itself as Ellen who, wrapped in the Policeman's jacket, was being escorted home. Another moved out from among the trees and was seen to be a solid mass comprising Miss Lark and the Professor, with the two dogs huddling against them, as though anxious not to be seen.

"Goodnight, all!" chirruped Miss Lark, as she spied the little group. "And *what* a good night!" She waved at the sky. "Did you ever see such a sparkle, Professor?"

The Professor tilted back his head. "Dear me! Someone seems to be setting off fireworks. Can this be the Fifth of November?"

"Goodnight," called Jane and Michael shrilly, and looked, for the first time, upwards. They had been so intent on the darkness around them and the changes the night had wrought in the earth, that they had forgotten the sky. But the blaze above them, of stars that bent so bright and near – the party evidently in full swing – that too was the work of the night. True, the night had created the frightening shapes but then, as though to make amends, had changed them into familiar figures. And what but the night was bringing them, with each turn of the perambulator's wheel, each best foot – left or right – thrust forward, to the place from which they had started?

Ahead of them, beyond the line of cherry trees, lights began to appear – not so bright as the ones above but, for all that, bright enough. It seemed as though each house in the Lane, leaning so closely to the next, had lit itself from its neighbour. There were constellations both below and above, the earth and the sky were next door to each other.

"Now, no more day-dreaming, Professor. We want our supper. So do the dogs." Miss Lark seized the arm of her friend, who was raptly gazing into the darkness.

"My dear Miss Wren, I am *not* day-dreaming. I am looking at a fallen star. See! Over there, on that lady's hat." He swept the newspaper from his head and bowed to Mary Poppins.

Miss Lark put on her lorgnette.

"Nonsense, Professor! Falling stars just fizzle out. They never reach the earth. That's just a common pigeon feather – covered with luminous paint, or something. Magicians use things like that for their tricks."

And she whisked him through the Lane Gate.

"Is that you, Professor?" called Mr Banks, racing full tilt along the Lane, with Mrs Banks at his heels.

The Professor looked uncertain. "I suppose it is. People tell me so. I'm never quite sure myself."

"Well, I've glorious news. I've found a new star!"

"You mean the one on that hat? I've seen it."

"No, no! On the Belt, my dear chap. Up till now it has had just three – a trio of shiners in a row. But, tonight, I've distinctly seen a fourth."

"Miss Partridge says it's just luminous paint."

"Paint? Absurd! You can't put paint on the sky, man! It's there, as large as life – and solid. I've verified it. So has Admiral

Boom. We've looked at it through his telescope. And who's Miss Partridge, anyway?"

"Lark!" said Miss Lark. "Do remember, Professor!"

"No, no, it's not just a lark! He means it. He's seen it through a telescope and telescopes don't lie."

"Of course they don't. They reveal facts. So, we're off to the Planetarium. The news must be spread abroad."

"But, George, the children!" Mrs Banks broke in.

"Don't worry. They're all right, I tell you. Put on a hat and I'll change my tie." Mr Banks was panting with excitement. "Perhaps they'll call it after me. Imagine it! Fame at last! A heavenly body by the name of Banks!"

And the happy astronomer dashed away, dragging Mrs Banks by the hand, to the door of his own house.

"Why Banks, I wonder? I always thought his name was Cooper. And I could have sworn it was hat, not belt. But my memory is not what it was – if, indeed, it was ever what it was." Vague and perplexed, yet still hopeful, the Professor looked round for his fallen star.

But Miss Lark was having no more nonsense. She took her friend firmly by the arm and hurried him off to supper.

The Professor, however, need not have worried. His memory was what it had been. His fallen star, even now, was making its way towards the Lane Gate. The feather glowed among the daisies and its light was reflected in the pairs of cherries that hung below the hat brim.

Jane and Michael looked up at it and then from the feather to the sky. Half dazzled by the resplendent light, they searched for, and found, what they sought. Ah, there! They needed no telescope to tell them.

Among the celestial ornaments, Orion's Belt gleamed on its unseen wearer – three large stars in a slanting line, and beside them, small, modest, but bright as a glow-worm, a fourth piece of bric-a-brac!

Neither the feather nor the extra star had been there when they set out. Their adventure had, indeed, been true. At last they could not believe it. And, meeting Mary Poppins' eyes, they knew that she knew what they knew. All things, indeed, were possible – sky-light upon an earthy hat-brim, earth-light on a skyey girdle.

They craned their necks as they straggled beside her, and gazed at the conflagration. How was the party going, they wondered. Was someone strutting in his new-found sparkle; another boasting of his elegant mittens; the other displaying their treasure-trove? And was there anyone up there to remind them, with a toss of the head, that handsome was as handsome did? No! There was only one such person and she was walking between them.

Behind them, Mr Twigley's bird burst into song again. Before them lay the Lane Gate. And as the perambulator creaked towards it they could see a necklace of shining windows beyond the cherry trees. The front door of Number Seventeen, left open by their excited parents, threw a long light down the garden path, as if to welcome them.

"Mary Poppins," said Jane, as they pushed their way on the

last lap of the day's excursion. "What will you do with your earrings?"

"Eat them," said Mary Poppins promptly. "Along with a cup of strong tea and a slice of buttered toast." What else were cherries for, after all?

"And what about my string bag?" Michael hugged her sleeve.

"Kindly do not swing on my arm. I am not a garden gate, Michael!"

"But where is it? Tell me!" he demanded. Was Pegasus, even now, he wondered, munching a meal of Coltsfoot?

Her shoulders went up with their characteristic shrug.

"String bags – pooh! – they're two a penny. Lose one and you can get another."

"Ah! But perhaps it's not lost!" He gave her a darting, sidelong glance. "And neither will you be, Mary Poppins, when you skedaddle off."

She drew herself up, insulted.

"I'll thank you, Michael Banks, to mind your manners. I am not in the habit of skedaddling."

"Oh, yes, you are, Mary Poppins," said Jane. "One day here and the next day gone, without a Word of Warning."

"But she's not nowhere, even so. And neither is my string bag," said Michael. "But where? Where, Mary Poppins?" Every place, surely, had a name! "How shall we know how to find you?"

They held their breaths, waiting for an answer. She looked at them for a long time and her blue eyes sparkled with it.

They could see it dance on to her tongue, all agog to make its disclosure. And then – it danced away. Whatever the secret was, she would keep it.

"Ah!" she said. And smiled.

"Ah! Ah! Ah! Ah!" repeated the Nightingale from its branch.

And above, from every quarter of the sky, there came an echoing "Ah!" The whole world was ringing with the riddle. But nothing, and nobody, answered it.

They might have known! She would not tell them. If she had never explained before, why should she do so now?

Instead, she gave them her haughty glance.

"I know where you two will be in a minute. And that's into bed, spit-spot!"

They laughed. The old phrase made them feel warm and secure. And even if there was no answer, there had been a reply. Earth and sky, like neighbours chatting over a fence, had exchanged the one same word. Nothing was far. All was near. And bed, they now realised, was exactly where they wanted to be, the safest place in the world.

Then Michael made a discovery.

"Well, bed's somewhere!" he exclaimed, surprised at his own cleverness. Plain, ordinary bed was Somewhere. He had never thought of that before! *Everything* had to be somewhere.

"And so will you be, Mary Poppins, with your carpet bag and parrot umbrella, sniffing and being important!"

He gave her a mischievous, questioning glance, daring her to deny it.

"And well-brought-up and respectable too!" Jane added her teasing to his.

"Impudence!"

She swung her handbag at them, and missed.

For already they were darting away to what was waiting for them.

Wherever she was, she would not be lost. That was answer enough.

"Somewhere! Somewhere! Somewhere!" they cried.

And, leaving the dark Park behind, they ran, laughing, across the Lane, through the gate and up the path and into the lighted house...

A.M.G.D.

THE HERBS IN THE STORY

and their botanical, local and Latin names

SOUTHERNWOOD Old man, Lad's love *Artemisia abrotanum*

LAVENDER *Lavandula vera*

MONEYWORT Creeping Jenny, Herb twopence
Lysimachia nummularia

SWEET BASIL *Ocimum basilicum*

DANDELION Dens leonis, Swine's snout *Taraxacum
officinale*

CHAMOMILE *Anthemis nobilis*

HONEYSUCKLE Woodbind *Lonicera caprifolium*

FOXGLOVE Folk's glove, Fairy thimbles *Digitalis
purpurea*

PARSLEY *Petroselinum crispum*

FENNEL *Foeniculum vulgare*

SOLOMON'S SEAL Lady's seals *Polygonatum multiflorum*

COLTSFOOT Ass's foot, Coughwort *Tussilago farfara*

GOOSEBERRY Feverberry, Goosegogs *Ribes grossularia*

RAMPION *Campanula rapunculus*

CUCUMBER Cowcumber *Cucumis sativus*

HEARTSEASE Love-in-idleness, Herb constancy *Viola
tricolor*

LEMON BALM Herb livelong *Melissa officinalis*

ELDER Pipe tree, Black elder *Sambucus nigra*

ROSEMARY Polar plant, Compass-weed *Rosmarinus
officinalis*

FORGET-ME-NOT *Myosotis symphytifolia*

ST JOHN'S WORT	All heal *Hypericum perforatum*
MARIGOLD	Ruddes, Mary Gowles, Oculis Christi *Calendula officinalis*
CORIANDER	*Coriandrum sativum*
CORNFLOWER	Bluebow, Bluebottle, Hurtsickle *Centaurea cyanis*
MARJORAM	Knotted Margery *Origanum majorana*
RUE	Herb of grace, Herbygrass *Ruta graveolens*
GOOD KING HENRY	Goosefoot, Fat hen *Chenopodium Bonus Henricus*
SWEET CICELY	Chervil, Sweet fern *Myrrhis odorata*
ROCKET	Dame's violet, Vesper flower *Hesperis matronalis*
BRACKEN	Brake fern, Female fern *Pteris aquilana*
MISTLETOE	Birdlime mistletoe, Herbe de la Croix *Viscum album*
LOVAGE	*Levisticum officinale*
CYCLAMEN	Sowbread *Cyclamen hederaefolium*
SORREL	Cuckoo's meat, Sour suds *Rumex acetosa*

Mary Poppins
and the House Next Door

To Bruno

CRACK! WENT THE teacup against the bowl of soapsuds. Mrs Brill, washing the china, scrabbled among the sparkling bubbles and fished it up in two pieces.

"Ah well," she said, as she tried, and failed, to fit them together. "It's needed somewhere else, I suppose." And she flung the two halves, with their twined roses and forget-me-nots, into the dustbin.

"Where?" demanded Michael. "Where will it be needed?" Who would need a broken cup? he wondered. It seemed a silly idea.

"How should I know?" fussed Mrs Brill. "It's an old saying, that's all. Now, you get along with your bit of work, and sit yourself down while you do it so that nothing else gets broken."

Michael settled himself on the floor and took the dishes as she handed them to him, drying them with the tea-towel and sighing as he did so.

Ellen had one of her dreadful colds, Robertson Ay was asleep on the lawn and Mrs Banks was taking an afternoon rest on the sofa in the drawing-room.

"As usual," Mrs Brill had complained, "no one to give me a helping hand."

"Michael will," Mary Poppins had said, seizing a tea-towel and thrusting it at him. "And the rest of us will go shopping and bring home the groceries. That will help."

"Why me?" Michael had grumbled, kicking a chair leg. He would like to have kicked Mary Poppins but that he would never have dared. For fetching the groceries was a special treat because, whenever the bill was paid, the grocer gave each of them – even Mary Poppins – a tasty liquorice stick.

"Well, why *not* you?" said Mary Poppins, giving him one of her fierce blue looks. "Jane did it last time. And somebody has to help Mrs Brill."

He knew there was no answer to that. If he mentioned liquorice, he would only get a short, sharp sniff. And anyway, even the King, he supposed, had sometimes to dry a dish or two.

So he kicked another leg of the chair, watching Mary Poppins as, with Jane carrying a string bag and the Twins and Annabel huddled into the perambulator, she went away down the garden path.

"Don't polish them. We haven't time for that. Just dry them and put them in a pile," Mrs Brill advised him.

So there he sat by the heaped-up dishes, forced into doing a kindly act and not feeling kind at all.

And after a time – it seemed like years to Michael – they all came back, laughing and shouting and, sure enough, sucking liquorice sticks. Jane gave him one, hot from her hand.

"The grocer sent it specially to you. And somebody's lost the tin of cocoa."

"Somebody?" Mary Poppins said tartly. "You, Jane, were carrying the bag! Who else could that somebody be?"

"Well, perhaps it just dropped out in the Park. I could go and look for it, Mary Poppins."

"Not now. What's done is done. Somebody loses, somebody finds. Besides, it's time for tea."

And she gathered the little ones out of the perambulator and hurried them all up the stairs before her.

In no time they were sitting round the Nursery table waiting for hot buttered toast and cake. Except for the liquorice sticks, everything was the same as usual. Mary Poppins' parrot-headed umbrella, her hat, which today had a pink rose in it, her gloves and her handbag were neatly in their places. The children were all neatly in theirs. And Mary Poppins was going about her afternoon's work like a neat and orderly whirlwind.

"It's just like any other day," said Number Seventeen to itself, as it listened to the familiar sounds and felt the familiar movements.

But Number Seventeen was wrong, for at that moment the doorbell rang and Mrs Brill came bustling into the drawing-room with a yellow envelope in her hand.

"Telegram!" she announced excitedly to Mrs Banks. "Your Aunt Flossie's broken her leg, maybe, or it could be something worse. I don't trust telegrams."

Mrs Banks took it with a trembling hand. She didn't trust

telegrams either. They always seemed to bring bad news.

She turned the envelope over and over.

"Well, aren't you going to open it?" Mrs Brill was eager to know the worst.

"Oh, I don't think I will," said Mrs Banks. "I'd rather wait until my husband comes home. It is addressed to him, anyway. See – 'George Banks, Seventeen Cherry Tree Lane.'"

"Well, if it's urgent, you'll be sorry you waited. A telegram is everyone's business."

Mrs Brill reluctantly left the room. She would have enjoyed hearing bad news.

Mrs Banks eyed the yellow envelope, as it stood there on the mantelpiece, leaning against a photograph and coolly keeping its secret.

"Perhaps," she said hopefully to herself, "it's good news, after all. Mrs Brill doesn't know everything."

But she couldn't help wishing that this might be one of the days when Mr Banks came home early.

And, as it happened, it was.

He had got off the bus at the end of the Lane and was sauntering home past Number Twenty-one – Admiral Boom's house that was built like a ship – past Twenty with its honeysuckle hedge, past Nineteen with the fish pond in the garden, until he came to Number Eighteen.

And there he stopped, full of surprise, and not altogether pleased. Around the gate his neighbours were gathered, all talking earnestly together. The Admiral and Mrs Boom, Mr Twenty and Mrs Nineteen and Miss Lark from Number

Sixteen. There was nothing odd in this, of course, a gathering of friends.

But what stopped Mr Banks in his tracks was the sight of a red-and-white striped tent, the kind that is put over open drains and other holes in the road. And beside it stood a brawny workman deep in conversation with the little group of neighbours.

"Ah, there you are, Banks, ship ahoy!" The Admiral's loud voice hailed him. "You're just the one to find out what this fellow thinks he's doing."

"I don't think, I know," said the workman mildly. "I'm looking over this here house to see what repairs it needs."

"But it's empty," Mr Banks said quickly. "It's been empty for years and years."

"Well, it won't be empty for long," said the man. "There's tenants coming in."

"But that's impossible." Mr Banks was distressed. "We all like it just as it is. Every street should have its deserted house."

"What for?"

"Well," began Mr Banks, a trifle uneasily, "so that people can fill it with their own ideas, the kind of neighbours they would like to have. We don't want just anyone, you know."

There was a murmur of assent from them all as they thought of the long-empty rooms of their dear Number Eighteen.

For the Admiral they were inhabited by a sea captain who had sailed with Nelson and was ready at any moment, no matter what the weather, to heave up the anchor and put to sea.

Mrs Boom saw it as the home of a little girl with straight

brown hair, the kind of child she would like to have had, who wandered about it, soft as a moth, humming gently to herself.

Mr Twenty, whose wife would never play chess with him, had friends there who were human chessmen – black and white kings and queens, bishops marching from corner to corner, knights riding up and down the stairs.

Mrs Nineteen, who was rather romantic, believed that in the empty house lived the grandmother she had never seen, telling wonderful bedtime stories, knitting pretty garments for her and always wearing silver slippers, even in the morning.

For Miss Lark, from Number Sixteen – the grandest dwelling in the Lane – it was the home of another dog exactly like Andrew, an aristocratic little dog who would never choose, as Andrew had done, a vulgar friend like Willoughby.

As for Mr Banks, he liked to think that in the attic of Number Eighteen, lived an old wise man with a very special telescope which, when you looked through its round glass eye, could show you what the universe was up to.

"Anyway," he said to the workman, "it's probably not fit to live in after being empty for so long. Have you examined the drains?"

"All of them in perfect condition."

"Well, the chimneys. Full of starlings' nests, I'll be bound."

"Clean as a whistle," said the man.

"What about the furniture? Mice making tunnels in the beds. Cockroaches in the kitchen."

"Not a mouse, Not a 'roach."

"And the dust. It must be everywhere, inches thick."

"Whoever comes into this house," said the man, "won't even need a duster. Everything's as good as new. And anyway," he began to dismantle his red-and-white tent, "houses are for human beings, not harum-scarum fancies."

"Well, if it must be, it must be," sighed Miss Lark. "Come, Andrew, come Willoughby, we will go home." And she walked away dejectedly, the two dogs at her heels looking equally depressed.

"You should have gone to sea," said the Admiral, looking ferociously at the workman.

"Why?"

"A sailor would stay on the deck of his ship and not come making trouble for those who live on the land."

"Can't bear the sea, it makes me seasick. And anyway, it's no fault of mine. I have me orders, 'to be carried out forthwith', I was told. The tenants are coming in tomorrow."

"Tomorrow!" everyone exclaimed. This was terrible.

"Let us go home," coaxed Mrs Boom. "Binnacle is making curry for supper. You'll like that, won't you, dear?"

Binnacle was a retired pirate who daily kept everything shipshape in Admiral Boom's ship-shaped house.

"Well, heave up the anchor and sail away, shipmates. There's nothing else to do."

The Admiral took Mrs Boom's arm and slouched off along the Lane, followed by Mrs Nineteen and Mr Twenty, both looking forlorn.

"A queer lot you are, I must say." The workman gathered up tent and tools. "All this to-do over an empty house!"

"You don't understand," said Mr Banks. "For us, it's not empty, far from it." And he turned towards his home.

Across the Lane, he could hear the Park Keeper doing his rounds. "Observe the Rules. Remember the Bye-laws." The starling on the top of Number Seventeen's chimney was giving his usual starling shriek. Laughter and shouting came from the Nursery mingled with the comments of Mary Poppins. He could hear Ellen's endless sneezing, the clatter of dishes in the kitchen, the sleepy snores of Robertson Ay – all the familiar sounds of home, everything the same as usual, comfortable, intimate.

But now, he thought, everything would be different.

"I have news for you," he said glumly, as Mrs Banks met him at the door.

"And I have news for *you*," she said. "There's a telegram on the mantelpiece."

He took the yellow envelope, ripped it open, read the message and was suddenly very still.

"Well, don't just stand there, George! Say something! Has anything happened to Aunt Flossie?" Mrs Banks was anxious.

"It is not Aunt Flossie. Aunt Flossie doesn't send telegrams. I will read it to you:

> "*Coming to live at Number Eighteen.*
> *Arriving 4.30 tomorrow. Bringing Luti.*
> *No help required.*"

Mr Banks paused for a moment. "It is signed," he said,

"Euphemia Andrew."

Mrs Banks gave a little shriek.

"Miss Andrew! Oh, I can't believe it. Our dear Number Eighteen!"

For Mrs Banks too had a friend in the house, a lady very much like herself who, when Mrs Brill took long days off to see her cousin's niece's baby or Ellen had one of her fearful colds or Robertson Ay fell asleep in the rosebed, would throw up her arms when she heard the news and say, "Oh, how dreadful! How will you manage?"

This Mrs Banks found a great comfort. Now she must face her troubles alone.

"And Luti!" she cried. "Who could that be?"

"Probably not who but what. One of her medicines, perhaps."

Mr Banks sat down on a chair and put his head in his hands. Miss Andrew had been his governess when he was a little boy, a lady who, though strong as a camel, took medicines by the dozen; a lady so strict, so stern, so forbidding that everyone knew her as the Holy Terror. And now, she, of all people, was coming to live next door to him in a house that was full of his dreams.

He looked at the telegram. "No help required. Well, that's a blessing. I won't have to light a fire in her bedroom as I did that time she came to stay and disappeared so suddenly and went off to the South Seas."

"I wish she had stayed there," said Mrs Banks. "But come, dear, we must tell the children."

"I wish I were in the South Seas myself. Anywhere but here."

"Now, George, don't be gloomy!"

"Why not? If a man can't be gloomy in his own house, where can he be gloomy, I'd like to know?" Mr Banks sighed heavily as he followed his wife up the front stairs looking like a man whose familiar world has fallen in pieces around him.

The Nursery was in an uproar. Annabel was banging her spoon on the table, John and Barbara, the Twins, were trying to push each other off their chairs, Jane and Michael were wrangling over the last piece of toast.

"Is this a Nursery or a cageful of monkeys?" Mary Poppins was asking in her sternest voice.

"A cageful of..." Michael was about to be daring when the door suddenly opened.

"We have news for you all," said Mrs Banks. "A telegram has come."

"Who from?" demanded Jane.

"Miss Andrew. You remember Miss Andrew?"

"The Holy Terror!" shouted Michael.

"Hush! We must always be polite. She is coming to live at Number Eighteen."

"Oh, no!" protested both the children. For they did indeed remember Miss Andrew, and how she had once come to stay and had disappeared so strangely.

"But it's ours!" cried Michael. "Number Eighteen belongs to us. She can't come and live there!" He was almost in tears.

"I'm afraid she can," said Mrs Banks. "Tomorrow. Bringing

someone or something whose name is Luti. And," she added coaxingly, "we must all be polite and kind, mustn't we? Mary Poppins, you'll see that they are neat and tidy and ready to greet her, won't you?" She turned timidly to Mary Poppins who was standing as still as a doorpost. It would have been impossible to tell what she was thinking.

"And when," she said acidly, looking as haughty as a duchess, "were they anything but neat and tidy?" The idea was quite absurd.

"Oh, never, never," fluttered Mrs Banks, feeling as she always did with Mary Poppins as though she were a very small girl instead of the mother of five children. "But you know how fussy Miss Andrew is! George!" She turned anxiously to her husband. "Don't you want to say something?"

"No," said Mr Banks fiercely. "I don't want to say *anything*."

And Mrs Banks, having delivered the unfortunate news, took her husband's hand and led him away.

"But I've got a friend who lives there," said Michael. "Gobbo, the clown we saw at the circus, who makes everybody laugh and looks so sad himself."

"I think the Sleeping Beauty's there, lying under a lacy quilt with a spot of blood on her finger." Jane too had her dreams of the house.

"She can't be," Michael protested. "There's no wall of thorns around it."

"There's nettles. They are just as good. Mary Poppins!" Jane turned to the motionless figure. "Who do *you* think lives in Number Eighteen?"

Mary Poppins sniffed. "Five, nice, quiet, well-behaved children – not like some people I could mention."

Her blue eyes were sternly blue but in their depths was the glint of a twinkle.

"Well, if they're so perfect they don't need a Mary Poppins. It's we who need you," Michael teased her. "Perhaps you'll make *us* perfect."

"Humph," she retorted. "That's not very likely."

"Everyone needs her." Jane patted her hand, hoping to tease her into a smile.

"Humph," said Mary Poppins again. But the smile appeared as she met her reflection in the glass. Of course, each seemed to be telling the other, everyone needed Mary Poppins. How could it be otherwise?

Then the two mirrored faces resumed their sternness.

"Now, no more argle-bargling. Spit-spot and into bed with you!"

And, for once, without argle-bargling, they did as they were told.

Much had happened. They needed to think it over, and were glad when their cheeks met the softness of their pillows, glad of the comforting warmth of the blankets.

Michael was thinking of Gobbo, Jane of the Sleeping Beauty. Their shadowy shapes would disappear from Number Eighteen and the solid figure of Miss Andrew would haunt the house instead.

"I wonder," said Jane thoughtfully, "exactly what a Luti is?" She had never heard the word before.

"Perhaps it's an animal," said Michael. "Maybe a kangaroo."

"Or a monkey – a Luti monkey. I would like that," said Jane.

And they fell asleep dreaming of a kangaroo, or perhaps a monkey, gambolling happily about the Lane among the Cherry Trees.

But it was neither a kangaroo, nor a monkey, as they were to learn next day.

It was Saturday. Number Eighteen looked naked and a little lonely without its surrounding hedge of nettles. A workman had come in the early hours, cut them down and carted them off.

The Banks family spent a nervous morning, and as the afternoon drew on, Mr Banks, like an anxious general, marshalled his troops at the front gate.

"We must be there to greet her," he said. "One has to be polite."

"Don't keep fussing, dear," said Mrs Banks. "Perhaps she won't stay long."

Jane and Michael looked at each other remembering how, on her last visit, Miss Andrew had come and gone so quickly, and the curious part Mary Poppins had played in that curious departure.

They glanced at her as she stood beside them, rocking the Twins and Annabel in the perambulator, her face rosy and serene. What was she thinking? They would never know.

"There she is!" cried Mr Banks, as a hansom cab, hung about with Gladstone bags, turned from the main road into the Lane. "She always travels with mountains of luggage. Goodness knows what is in it."

They all watched, holding their breaths, as the cabhorse wearily clopped along, dragging its heavy load – past Miss Lark's house, past the little group anxiously waiting outside Number Seventeen.

"Whoa, there," said the cabman, tugging at the reins, and the curious conveyance came to a stop at the gate of the empty house. He clambered down from his high seat and removed several Gladstone bags that hung from the roof of the cab. Then he opened the door and hauled out a large black leather trunk.

"Carefully, please, there are breakables in it," cried a haughty, familiar voice from within. A black-booted foot appeared on the step, then slowly, the rest of Miss Andrew, a large, ungainly, cumbersome figure, lumbered out on to the pavement.

She glanced around, and spied the family group.

"Well, George, I am glad you have not forgotten your manners. I expected you to meet me."

"Welcome, Miss Andrew!" Mr and Mrs Banks were rigidly polite.

"And the children seem clean and tidy enough. I hope their behaviour matches their appearance."

Miss Andrew craned her head and at the sight of the neat blue-coated figure standing in the background, she shrank back nervously.

"I see," she said, her voice trembling on the words, "that

you still have the same young person taking charge of your household. Well, all I can say is, I hope she gives satisfaction."

"She does indeed," said Mr Banks, with a bow towards the blue coat.

"Welcome, Miss Andrew," said Mary Poppins, in a voice Jane and Michael had never heard – sweet, shy and unassuming. Miss Andrew turned her head away and her glance swept over the garden.

"Really, George, you live in a wilderness. Everything needs pruning. And what is that heap of garments doing in the middle of the lawn."

"That," Mr Banks said, "is Robertson Ay. He is taking a little rest."

"In the afternoon? Ridiculous! I hope you will take very good care that he never rests in *my* garden. Here," she turned, fumbling in her bag, to the heavily breathing cabman, "take the key and carry my luggage into the house."

"Well, I've just got to lever this here trunk." The man edged a chest through the door of the cab. "And then we can let out the little feller."

Jane and Michael looked at each other. Little feller! Did he mean a monkey or a kangaroo?

The chest fell with a thump to the pavement. It was followed by neither kangaroo, nor monkey, but by a small, strangely dressed boy, a little taller, perhaps, than Jane, with a large black bag in his hand. As he bent under the weight of it, they could see a round honey-coloured face with black hair falling loosely about it above a stiff white collar.

"Good Heavens!" said Mr Banks, in a whisper. "He's wearing my old clothes! She must have kept them all these years!"

The small figure, in knickerbockers, jacket and large brown boots stepped delicately down the step and stood there, hanging his head.

"This is Luti," pronounced Miss Andrew. "His name means Son of the Sun. He has come with me from the South Sea islands to get a good solid education and also to take care of me. Put down the medicine bag, Luti, and greet our next-door neighbours."

The bag was put down, the bent head lifted. And as he beheld the group at the gate a smile lit up the sunburnt face as the boy took a step towards it.

"Peace and blessings," he said shyly, spreading out his arms.

"That will do," said Miss Andrew sharply. "We don't use the island language here. Good afternoon is enough."

"And peace and blessings to *you*, Luti," Mr Banks cried heartily. "We are very glad to welcome you. There's a hole in the fence, just there," he pointed. "You can come through it any time. My children will be delighted to see you – won't you, Jane and Michael?"

"Oh, yes!" said Jane and Michael raptly. This was better than a kangaroo or monkey. It was a new friend to play with.

"George!" Miss Andrew's voice was like the snap of a whip. "Pray do not meddle in my affairs. Luti is here to work, not play. He will be busy with his lessons and making the porridge – we shall live on porridge, it is very nourishing – and getting my medicines ready. I intend him to be a credit to me so that when he eventually returns to the island he will go as something useful – a doctor or perhaps a teacher. In the meantime, we will continue our studies. And for relaxation, once a month, he and I *together*, George, will pay you a little visit. So go and waken your man, please, and tell him to repair the hole in the fence. We will have no to-ings and fro-ings between us. Is all the luggage safely in?"

She turned to the breathless cabman and gave him a coin as he nodded.

"Then pick up the medicine bag, Luti. We will go and inspect our new home."

She strode towards Number Eighteen and Luti, after a glance at Jane and Michael – they could not tell if it were sad or happy – shouldered his burden and followed her, and the front door closed behind them.

The children looked at Mary Poppins. Her face was the only cheerful one among them. But now her smile was mysterious as though she was sharing a secret with herself.

"We will go in to tea," she said briskly, giving the perambulator a push, "and then perhaps a game of Ludo."

Jane and Michael enjoyed playing Ludo. But today it had no interest for them. They had something else on their minds. They followed slowly, dragging their feet, thinking of the golden boy who had appeared for a brief moment and then had been taken away.

"That poor child!" murmured Mrs Banks, looking tearfully at her husband.

"Well I said she was a Holy Terror." Mr Banks sighed deeply as he turned to the jumbled heap on the lawn to waken the sleeping figure.

And all the inhabitants of the Lane who had been leaning over their gates watching, went quietly into their houses. Number Eighteen was no longer theirs. There was nothing more to be said.

The Lane was silent except for the voice of the Park Keeper, "Observe the Rules. Remember the Bye-laws." And nearer at hand, the sleepy yawns of Robertson Ay as he put a nail to the loose paling and gave it a blow with his hammer. That done, he slid down on to the grass and went to sleep again.

Presently, the nail fell out, the paling gave a sideways lurch, and the hole in the fence between the houses was as it had always been.

Early next morning, when the sun rose over the trees of the Park, the Lane was peacefully asleep, not even a bird stirred.

Even so, something stirred. Jane and Michael, one carrying a banana and the other an apple, were tiptoeing cautiously through the Nursery of Number Seventeen, past the camp-bed where Mary Poppins lay sleeping, as neat and uncrumpled as though she and the bed were objects in a shop window. They smiled triumphantly at each other – Mary Poppins would not notice them! But at that moment, she opened her eyes and her blue gaze fell upon them.

"And what do you two think you're doing?" She glanced at the fruit in their hands.

They jumped. She had woken, after all.

"Well, Mary Poppins," Michael spluttered. "How would *you* like to eat nothing but porridge?" He eyed her anxiously.

"We thought, Mary Poppins," Jane tried to explain. "We thought if we put some food down by the fence, Luti –" she nodded towards Number Eighteen – "might perhaps come and find it." She was as anxious as Michael.

Mary Poppins said nothing. She merely rose from her bed like a statue, leaving not a crease behind. Her hair hung in a plait down her back and her nightgown fell in neat folds around her as she stretched out her arm towards the door.

"Fetch me my handbag. It's hanging on the handle."

They ran eagerly to obey her and presently, sifting through the pockets, she took out of it a bar of chocolate and silently held it out. Michael made a rush at her and hugged her round the waist. He could feel her bony shape in his arms and her plait swung round his ears.

"Don't huggle and squeeze me like that, Michael Banks. I am not a Teddy Bear!"

"No, you're not," he cried delightedly. "You're better than a Teddy Bear."

"Anyone can have a Teddy Bear. But we have you, Mary Poppins," said Jane.

"Oh, indeed?" she said with an uppish sniff, as she loosened Michael's hold. "Well, there's having and having, I assure you! Now go downstairs quietly, please, you don't want to disturb the household." And she pushed them before her to the door and closed it softly behind them.

Sleep was all about them as they crept through the house, slid down the banisters and tiptoed out into the garden.

No sound came from Number Eighteen as they placed the fruit and the bar of chocolate on the crossbar of the fence.

And no sound came from it all the morning as they played among the trees and flowers until Mary Poppins called them to lunch. Even when they raced down again, the banana, the apple and the chocolate were still in the same position.

But then, as they turned away from the hole in the fence, a strange noise came from the house next door – a deep and rhythmic rumble that went on and on and on. Everyone in the Lane could hear it and the house seemed to tremble with it.

The lady in Number Nineteen, who was of a nervous disposition, was afraid it might be the beginning of a volcano. Mr Twenty gave it as his opinion that it was a lion snoring.

Jane and Michael, watching from the branches of the pear-tree in their back garden, felt that whatever it was, it must surely mean that something was going to happen.

And it did.

The front door of Number Eighteen opened and through it came a small figure, cautiously glancing from side to side. Slowly, he made his way round the house till he came to the hole in the fence, and then, seeing the fruit and the chocolate, he touched them with a delicate finger.

"They're for you!" shouted Jane, hurriedly scrambling down from her branch with Michael at her heels.

Luti looked up, a broad smile making his face like the sun, and he spread out his arms towards them.

"Peace and blessings!" he shyly whispered, cocking his head to one side, as he listened to the rumble.

"Missanda sleeps in the afternoon from two of the clock till three. So I came to see what these objects were."

It was not a volcano after all, not even a lion. The rumbling noise was Miss Andrew snoring.

"The fruit is from Jane and me," Michael told him, "and the chocolate from Mary Poppins."

"Mary Poppins?" Luti murmured the name to himself as though he were remembering something that he had long forgotten.

"There she is." Michael nodded to where Mary Poppins stood by the pear-tree, rocking Annabel in the perambulator.

"Peace and blessings to her," said Luti, waving his hand at the upright figure with the large pink rose in its hat. "I will hide these gifts within my pockets and eat them at night when I go to bed. Missanda eats only porridge."

"Is it a nice bed?" Jane enquired. She wanted to hear about everything that happened in Number Eighteen.

"Well, perhaps it is a little soft. On my island we do not sleep in beds but on mats that my mother weaves for us from the leaves of the coconut palm."

"You could lie on the floor," said Michael. "That would be almost as good."

"No, I must do as Missanda wishes. I am here to be of comfort to her, measure her many medicines, cook the porridge when the fire is hot and study my seven-times-seven. That my parents promised her, for they think she is a learnt person and will send me some day back to the island with knowledge of many things."

"But aren't you lonely?" Jane asked him. "And aren't they lonely for you?"

She was thinking how she herself would feel if Miss Andrew took her far away and of how her parents would grieve. No, no such thing could ever happen, not for all the knowledge in the world.

Luti's face crumpled. The smile faded.

"I am lonely for ever," his voice was husky. "But a promise has been made to her. If they have need of me, they will send—"

"A telegram!" exclaimed Michael. "In a yellow envelope." A telegram was always exciting.

"On the island we have no such things. But my Grandmother, Keria, said for my comfort, 'When we have need of you, it will be known.' She is a Wise Woman. She reads the stars and understands what the sea is saying. But, harken! I hear the bells singing!"

Luti put his hand to his ear as the church clock beyond the Park rang out. "One, Two, Three!" it said. And at the same moment the rumbling from Number Eighteen stopped, as though switched off.

"Missanda has woken from her sleep." Luti hurriedly gathered up fruit and chocolate and stuffed them into his pockets.

"Peace and blessings!" He raised his hand, his bright glance taking in Mary Poppins as well as Jane and Michael.

Then he turned and ran across the lawn, his feet in Mr Banks' big boots crushing the grass as he went.

A door opened and closed behind him and Number Eighteen, suddenly, was as soundless as it had always been.

But the next day, and all the days after it, promptly at two o'clock, the rumbling began again.

"Preposterous! Not to be borne! We must complain to the Prime Minister!" said the people in the Lane. But they knew that even the Prime Minister could no more stop somebody snoring than he could say "Halt!" to a snowstorm. They would just have to grin and bear it.

So that was what they did. And the grinning and bearing made them realise that Miss Andrew's snoring had its fortunate side. For now, between two and three o'clock, they could meet the smiling brown-faced stranger she had brought from the other side of the world. Otherwise, they would never have seen him, cooped up as he was, like a bird in a cage.

So, as well as the fruit that Jane and Michael put on the fence every afternoon – Mary Poppins always in the background – Luti soon found himself showered with gifts.

Mrs Nineteen gave him a paper fan, such as she would like to have made for the Grandmother she had never known.

Mr Twenty, a gruff, shy man, presented him with the King and Queen of an old chess set from his attic.

Admiral Boom, in a voice that would have roused from sleep anyone but Miss Andrew, hailed him with "Ahoy there, shipmate!" and pressed upon him a six-inch-long carved canoe, faded and shiny from spending years in the dark of a trouser pocket. "It's my mascot!" he explained. "Brought me luck all my life, ever since I was a midshipman sailing the South Seas."

Binnacle, the retired pirate, gave him a dagger with a broken point. "It's me second-best," he apologised, "but it'll slit a throat or two if you're minded to become a pirate."

Luti had no desire to become a pirate, far less to slit anyone's throat, but he took the dagger with gratitude and hid it carefully inside his jacket in case Miss Andrew should see it.

The Park Keeper too had a present for him – a page out of an exercise book on which he had printed in large letters, "Observe the Rules. Remember the Bye-laws".

"You'll need this," he said earnestly, "if you ever get to come to the Park."

Luti spelled out the strange words. "What is a Bye-law?" he wanted to know.

The Park Keeper scratched his head. "I don't rightly know myself, but it's something you have to remember."

To remember something he did not know! This seemed like a riddle to Luti. But he put the paper into his pocket and decided to think about it.

Even Andrew and Willoughby from Number Sixteen, came each with a bone in his mouth. And when Luti opened the gate they deposited the bones before him, and walked home waving their tails proudly and feeling noble and generous.

"Peace and blessings!" said Luti, smiling – which was what he said to everyone – and hid the bones under the hedge so that some day another dog would find them.

Everyone wanted to know him. If they had lost Number Eighteen, they had been given a sun-browned stranger who for one hour, every day, smiled upon them and blessed them.

But the stolen hour was mostly spent with Jane and Michael at the hole in the fence, which seemed to be no longer a hole but a place where North and South met, and roses and columbines took the air with waving coconut palms.

Jane and Michael shared their toys, and taught Luti to play Ludo, while he made them whistles from leaves of grass, told them about the coral island and stories of his ancestors who came from the Land of the Sun. And of his Grandmother, Keria, who knew the language of birds and beasts and how to subdue a thunderstorm. Jane and Michael many times wished they had a Wise Woman for a grandmother. Aunt Flossie would never be able to deal with thunder. All she could do was escape from it by getting under a bed.

And always, as if by chance – but they knew that nothing she did was by chance – Mary Poppins would be at hand, rocking Annabel to sleep, playing with John and Barbara, or sitting on the garden seat reading *Everything a Lady Should Know*.

But there came a day when the clock struck two and Jane and Michael went to the hole to find no Luti there.

It was Monday, and therefore Washing Day. It was also

dim and misty as though a cloud had swallowed the sun.

"Just my luck!" said Mrs Brill, as she pegged the sheets on the lines. "I need the sun, but it doesn't need me."

The mist did not bother Jane and Michael. They merely waited, peering through it, for a glimpse of a well-known figure. But when at last it did come, it was not the Luti they knew. He was bent and huddled like an old, old man, with his arms hugging his chest. And as he threw himself down beside them, they saw that he was weeping.

"What is it, Luti? We have brought you some pears. Don't you want to eat them?"

"No, no, I am troubled in my heart. Something is trying to speak to me. I can hear a knocking."

"Where?" They looked about uneasily. There was no sound anywhere but the rise and fall of Miss Andrew's snoring.

"In here." Luti beat his breast, rocking himself to and fro. "They are calling to me – knock, knock, knock! Keria said I would surely know. They are telling me to come home. Alas, what must I do?" He looked at the children, with streaming eyes. "The lady with the flower in her hat – she would understand."

"Mary Poppins!" Michael shouted. "Mary Poppins, where are you?"

"I am not deaf, nor in Timbuctoo. And you, Michael, are not a Hyena. Kindly speak more quietly. Annabel is asleep."

The hat with the pink rose bobbing on it leant over the top of the fence. "Tell me, what is the matter, Luti?" Mary Poppins looked down at the sobbing child.

"I hear a knocking inside me, here." Luti put his hand on his heart. "I think they are sending for me."

"Then the moment has come for you to go home. Climb through the hole and follow me."

"But Missanda – her porridge, her medicines, and my learning of many things!" Luti eyed her anxiously.

"Miss Andrew will be taken care of," said Mary Poppins firmly. "Come with me, all of you. There is not much time."

Jane and Michael helped the half-willing boy hurriedly through the gap. And Mary Poppins took his hand, placing it closely beside her own on the handle of the perambulator, as the little procession made its way through a corridor of wet white sheets.

They were all silent as they hurried through the misty garden, across the Lane where the ripe cherries hung from the branches, each cluster veiled in white, and into the Park with its hazy shapes of bushes, trees and swings.

The Park Keeper, like an eager dog, came lolloping towards them. "Observe the Rules. Remember the Bye-laws! You've got it on your piece of paper," he said, looking at Luti.

"Observe them yourself," said Mary Poppins. "There's some wastepaper over there. Put it in the litter bin."

The Park Keeper turned sulkily away and went towards the litter. "Who does she think she is?" he muttered. But no answer came to his question.

Mary Poppins marched on, stopping only at the edge of the Lake to admire her own reflection, with its misty rose-bedecked hat and the wide knitted scarf with its matching roses that today she wore round her shoulders.

"Where are we going, Mary Poppins?" Where *could* they go in the mist, thought Jane.

"Walk up, walk up!" said Mary Poppins. And it seemed to the children that she was herself walking up, putting her foot upon the cloud as if it were a staircase and tilting up the perambulator as though climbing a hill.

And suddenly, they were all climbing, leaving the Park behind them, walking upon the misty substance that seemed as firm as a snowdrift. Luti leant against Mary Poppins as though she were the one safe thing in the world, and together they pushed the perambulator while Jane and Michael followed.

"Observe the Rules!" the Park Keeper shouted. "You can't climb the clouds. It's against the Bye-laws! I shall have to inform the Prime Minister."

"Do!" Mary Poppins called over her shoulder, as she led them higher and higher.

On they went, ever upwards, with the mist growing firmer at every step and the sky around them brighter. Till at last, as though they had come to the top of a staircase, a gleaming cloud-field had spread out before them as flat and white as a plate. The sun lay across it in stripes of gold and, to the children's astonishment, a huge full moon confronted them, anchored, as it were, at the edge of a cloud.

It was crowded with objects of every description – umbrellas, handbags, books, toys, luggage, parcels, cricket bats, caps, coats, slippers, gloves, the kind of things people leave behind them in buses or trains or on seats in a park.

And among these varied articles, with a small iron cooking stove beside it, stood an old battered armchair, and in the chair sat a bald-headed man in the act of raising a cup to his lips.

"Uncle! Stop! Don't you dare drink it!" Mary Poppins' voice rang out sharply and the cup banged down into its saucer.

"What, what? Who? Where?" With a start, the man lifted his head. "Oh, it's you, Mary! You gave me a fright. I was just going to take a sip of cocoa."

"You were, indeed, and you know quite well that cocoa makes one sleepy!" She leant in and took the cup from his hand.

"It's not fair," grumbled the uncle. "Everyone else can indulge themselves with a soothing drink. But not me, not the poor Man-in-the-Moon. He has to stay awake night and day to keep a watch on things. And anyway, people should be more careful and not go losing tins of cocoa – yes, and cups to put the cocoa in."

"That's our cup!" Michael exclaimed. "Mrs Brill said when she broke it that it would be needed somewhere else."

"Well, it was. So I glued the bits together. And then someone dropped a tin of cocoa." He glanced at the tin on the edge of the stove and Jane remembered that such a one had fallen from the string bag on their way home from the grocer's.

"And I had a packet of sugar by me, so you see, with three such treats coming together, I just couldn't resist them. I'm sorry, Mary. I won't do it again, I promise." The Man-in-the-Moon looked shamefaced.

"You won't get the chance," said Mary Poppins, seizing the tin from the top of the stove and stuffing it into her handbag.

"Well, goodbye cocoa, goodbye sleep!" The Man-in-the-Moon sighed heavily. Then he grinned and looked at Jane and Michael. "Did you ever know anyone like her?" he asked.

"Never, never!" they both replied.

"Of course you didn't," he beamed proudly. "She's the One and Only."

"Do all lost things come to the Moon?" Jane thought of the lost things in the world and wondered if there was room for them.

"Mostly, yes," said the Man-in-the-Moon. "It's a kind of storehouse."

"And what's at the back of it?" asked Michael. "We only see this side."

"Ah, if I knew that, I'd know a lot. It's a mystery, a kind of riddle – a front without a back you might say, as far as I'm concerned. Besides, it's very overcrowded. You couldn't relieve me of anything, could you? Something you might have lost in the Park?"

"I can!" said Jane suddenly, for among the parcels and umbrellas she had spied a shabby, familiar shape.

"The Blue Duck!" She reached for the faded toy. "The Twins dropped it out of the perambulator."

"And there's my dear old mouth organ." Michael pointed to a metal shape on the shelf above the stove. "But it doesn't make music any more. It's really no use to me."

"Nor to me, either. I have tried it. A musical instrument that can't make music! Take it, there's a good fellow, and put it in your pocket."

Michael reached for the mouth organ and as he did so, something that was lying beside it toppled sideways and came bouncing down, rolling out over the cloud.

"Oh, that is mine, my lost coconut!" Luti stepped out from behind Mary Poppins and seized the moving object. It was brown and shaggy, round as a ball, one side of it closely shaven with a round face carved upon it.

Luti hugged the hairy thing to his breast.

"My father carved it," he said proudly, "and I lost it one day in the tide of the sea."

"And now the tide has given it back. But you, young man, should be on your way. They are all waiting for you on the island and Keria is at her clay stove making spells with herbs for your safe return. Your father has lately hurt his arm and he needs your help in the canoe." The Man-in-the-Moon spoke firmly to Luti.

"He *is* on his way," said Mary Poppins. "That is why we are here."

"Ha! I knew you had something up your sleeve. You never visit me, Mary, my dear, just for a friendly cup of tea – or perhaps I should say cocoa!" The Man-in-the-Moon grinned impishly.

"I want you to keep an eye on him. He is young for such a long journey, Uncle."

"As if I could help it – you know that. Not a wink will I take, much less forty! Trust your old uncle, my girl."

"How do you know Keria?" asked Jane. The thought of the Wise Woman far away filled her with a kind of dream. She wished she could know her too.

"In the same way that I know everyone. It's my job to watch and wake. The world turns and I turn with the world; mountain and sea, city and desert; the leaf on the bough and the bough bare; men sleeping, waking, working; the cradle child, the old woman, the wise ones and the not so wise; you in your smock, Michael in his sailor blouse; the children on Luti's South Sea island in their girdles of leaves and wreaths of flowers such as he too will wear in the morning. Those things he has on now, Mary, would be most unsuitable."

"I have thought of that, thank you," said Mary Poppins, unfastening Luti's stiff collar and, with her usual lightning speed, sweeping off jacket and knickerbockers and Mr Banks' big boots. Then, as he stood there in his underwear, she wound about him, as one would a parcel, her knitted scarf with its pink roses that matched the one on her hat.

"But my treasures! I must take them with me." Luti eyed her earnestly.

Mary Poppins took from the perambulator a battered paper bag. "Fuss, fuss, fuss!" she said, with a sniff, as he fished in the pockets of his jacket.

"I could take care of the dagger for you." Michael was secretly envious. He had often had thoughts of becoming a pirate.

"One must never give away a gift. My father will use it for his carving and cutting twigs for the fire."

Luti stuffed the dagger into his bag with the fan, the wooden King and Queen and the Admiral's canoe. Last of all came a dark and sticky lump of something wrapped up in a handkerchief.

"The chocolate bar!" Jane exclaimed. "We thought you had eaten it up."

"It was too precious," said Luti simply. "We have no such sweetmeats on the island. They shall have a taste of it, all of them."

He reached an arm out of the scarf and stowed the bag in its woollen folds. Then he picked up the shaggy coconut, held it for a moment to his heart, before thrusting it at the children.

"Remember me, please," he said shyly. "I am indeed sad to leave you."

Mary Poppins picked up the folded clothes and laid them neatly on the floor of the moon.

"Come, Luti, it is time to go. I will show you the way. Jane and Michael, take care of the little one. Uncle, remember your promise."

She put her arm round the pink knitted bundle and Luti turned within it, smiling.

"Peace and blessings!" He held up his hand.

"Peace and blessings!" cried Jane and Michael.

"Do exactly as she tells you," said the Man-in-the-Moon, "and Peace and blessings, my boy!"

They watched him being marched away over the white cloudy field to the place where it met the sky. There Mary Poppins bent down to him, pointing to a string of cloudlets that floated like puffballs in the blue. They saw Luti nod as he gazed at them, saw him hold up his hand in a farewell gesture, then his bare legs took a little run that ended in an enormous leap.

"Oh, Luti!" they cried anxiously, and gasped with relief as he landed safely in the middle of the nearest puffball. Then he was skimming lightly across it and jumping on to the next. Oh, on he went, bounding over the gulfs of air between the floating clouds.

A shrill sound came back to them. He was singing, they could distinguish the words:

> "*I am Luti, Son of the Sun,*
> *I am wearing a garment of roses,*
> *I am going home to my island,*
> *Peace and blessings, O clouds!*"

Then he was silent and lost to sight. Mary Poppins was standing beside them and the moon, when they turned to look at it, was off on its course sailing away.

"Goodbye!" called Jane and Michael, waving. And the faint shape of an arm waved back with an answering call of "*Au Revoir!*".

Mary Poppins brandished her parrot-headed umbrella and then turned to the children. "Now, quick march and best foot forward!"

The pink rose bobbed jauntily on her hat as she gave the perambulator a twist and sent it rolling on a downward slope.

They seemed to be sliding rather than walking with the cloud growing mistier every second. Soon the shapes of trees loomed through the haze and suddenly, instead of air, there was solid earth beneath their feet and the Park Keeper and the Prime Minister were coming towards them, on the Long Walk, the emerging sun bright on their faces.

"There they are, just like I told you, coming right down out of the sky, breaking the Rules and the Bye-laws!"

"Nonsense, Smith, they had merely walked into the mist and now that it's lifted you can see them again. It has nothing to do with the Bye-laws. Good afternoon, Miss Mary Poppins. I must apologise for the Park Keeper. One would think, to hear him talk, that you had been visiting the Moon, ha, ha!"

The Prime Minister laughed at his own joke.

"One would indeed!" Mary Poppins replied, with a gracious, innocent smile.

"And what have you done with the other one?" the Park Keeper demanded. "The little brown fellow – left him up in the air?" He had seen Luti with the family troupe and now he was with it no longer.

The Prime Minister regarded him sternly. "Really, Smith, you go too far. How could anyone be left in the sky, supposing he could get there? You see, as we all do, shapes in the mist and your imagination runs away with you. Get on with your work in the Park, my man, and don't go molesting innocent people who are simply strolling through it. But now I must run away myself. They say there is trouble in the Lane. Someone appears to have lost their wits and I must look into it, I suppose. Good day to you, Miss Poppins. Next time you go climbing into the blue, pray give my respects to the Man-in-the-Moon!"

And, again laughing heartily, the Prime Minister swept off his hat and hurried away through the Park Gates.

Mary Poppins smiled to herself as she and the children followed closely behind him.

Angrily staring after them, the Park Keeper stood in the Long Walk. She had made a fool of him again! He was sure she had been up in the sky and he wished with all his heart she had stayed there.

There was, indeed, trouble in the Lane.

A large woman, with a big black bag in one hand, and tearing her hair with the other, was standing at the gate of Number Eighteen, alternately shouting and sobbing.

And Miss Lark's dogs, usually so quiet, were jumping up and down, barking at her.

Of course it was Miss Andrew.

Mary Poppins, cautiously walking on tiptoe, signalled to the children to do the same as they followed in the steps of the Prime Minister.

He was clearly nervous when he reached the scene.

"Er – is there anything, madam, I can do to help you?"

Miss Andrew seized him by the arm. "Have you seen Luti?" she demanded. "Luti has gone. I have lost Luti. Oh, oh, oh!"

"Well," the Prime Minister glanced around anxiously. "I am not quite sure what a Luti is."

It might, he thought, be a dog, or a cat, even, perhaps a parrot. "If I knew, I could, perhaps, be of use."

"He looks after me and measures my medicines and gives

them to me at the proper times."

"Oh, a chemist! No, I have seen no chemist. Certainly not a lost one."

"And he makes my porridge in the morning."

"A cook, then. No, I have not seen a cook."

"He comes from the South Seas and I've lost him!" Miss Andrew burst anew with sobs.

The Prime Minister looked astonished. A cook – or a chemist – from the South Seas! Such a one, if lost, would be hard to find.

"Well, give me your bag and we'll take a walk along the Lane. Somebody may have seen him. You, perhaps, madam," he said to Miss Lark, who was hurrying in pursuit of her dogs.

"No!" said Miss Lark. "Neither have Andrew and Willoughby!" She was not going to have anything to do with the woman whose snoring had disturbed the Lane.

The two dogs followed her, angrily growling. And the Prime Minister urged Miss Andrew along, letting her keep her grasp on his arm, as they went from gate to gate.

No, Mrs Nineteen had seen nothing. That was all she would say. And Mr Twenty repeated her words. Neither felt sympathy for Miss Andrew. She had taken their precious Number Eighteen and, moreover, had kept locked up within it, the sunny stranger who, for just one little hour a day, they had come to love and respect. If Luti were indeed lost they hoped that some better fate would find him.

"No, no, always no! Will nobody help me?" wailed Miss Andrew, grasping the Prime Minister more tightly.

And behind them, like a soundless shadow, the perambulator swept along, with Mary Poppins and Jane and Michael walking softly on the grass.

The Prime Minister's arm was beginning to ache as Miss Andrew, continually lamenting, drew him towards Binnacle's ship-shaped cottage which stood at the end of the Lane.

Binnacle was sitting on his front doorstep, playing his concertina and the Admiral, with Mrs Boom beside him, was singing at the top of his voice his favourite sea-shanty.

> "*Sailing, sailing, over the bounding main,*
> *And many a stormy wind shall blow*
> *Till Jack comes home again.*"

"Stop! Stop!" Miss Andrew shrieked. "Listen to what I have to tell you. Luti is lost. He has gone away."

The Admiral broke off in mid-song. The concertina was silent.

"Blast my gizzard! Lost, you say? I don't believe it – he's a sensible lad. He's probably simply up-anchored and gone to join the navy. That's what a sensible lad would do. Don't you think so, Prime Minister?"

Privately, the Prime Minister did not think so at all. The navy, he felt, had all the cooks and chemists it needed. But he knew from experience that if he disagreed with the Admiral he would be advised to go to sea and he preferred being a landlubber.

"Well, perhaps," he said uneasily, "we must enquire further."

"But what shall I do?" Miss Andrew broke in. "He's lost and I've nowhere to go!"

"You've Number Eighteen," Mrs Boom said gently. "Isn't that enough?"

"Ask Binnacle!" said Admiral Boom. "He has an extra cabin. Plenty of room for her and her chattels."

Binnacle glanced at the Admiral. Then he eyed Miss Andrew reflectively. "Well, I could manage the medicines and all pirates know how to cook porridge. But –" his voice now held a note of warning – "you've got to pay the price!"

Relief dawned on Miss Andrew's face. "Oh, anything! Ask any price you like. I will gladly pay it." She loosened her grasp on the Prime Minister's arm.

"Nah, nah, it's not the money. *You* need someone to cook and measure and *I* need someone to read to me – not once or twice but whenever I'm free!"

"Oh, I could think of nothing better." A smile made its way on to Miss Andrew's face, which was not used to smiling. "I have many books I could bring with me and teach you what I taught Luti."

"Look, lady. I don't want no 'eddication'. All a pirate needs to learn is how to be a pirate. But –" and again there was a note of warning – "I won't have anyone in my house unless they can be a proper shipmate and dance the Sailor's Hornpipe!"

"The Hornpipe!" Miss Andrew was shocked. "I could never think of such a thing. Besides, I don't even know it!"

"Of course you could!" said the Admiral. "Everyone on sea or land can do the Sailor's Hornpipe. All you need is to hear the music. Strike a chord, Binnacle. Up with the anchor!"

Binnacle grinned at the Admiral, and the concertina, at a touch of his hand, broke into the rocking tune.

The Admiral's feet began to twitch, so did Mrs Boom's. So did the Prime Minister's. And Mrs Nineteen and Mr Twenty, hearing the sound from their front gardens, began to sway with the music.

But Miss Andrew stood as if carved in stone, her face fierce and determined. 'Nothing will move me,' it seemed to say, 'not even an earthquake'.

Mary Poppins regarded her thoughtfully, as the music grew wilder and wilder. Then she plucked the mouth organ from Michael's pocket and put it to her lips.

Immediately a tune broke from it keeping time with the concertina. And slowly, slowly, as though against its will, the stone figure thrust from beneath its skirts two large feet that had never danced but were now beginning to shuffle. Heel and toe, away we go, across the bounding main.

And suddenly they were all sailors, Miss Andrew among them, unwillingly moving her great bulk through the measures of the hornpipe.

The Twins and Annabel bobbed up and down. Jane and Michael pranced beside them, while the Cherry Trees bent and bowed and the cherries twirled on their stems. Only Mary Poppins stood still, the mouth organ, held against her lips, giving out its lively tune.

Then it was over, the last chord played, and everyone – except Miss Andrew – was breathless and pleased with themselves.

"Bravo, messmate!" the Admiral roared, doffing his hat to the stony figure.

But the stony figure took no notice. It had caught sight suddenly of Mary Poppins, stuffing the mouth organ into Michael's pocket.

A long, long look, as of two wolves meeting, passed between the pair.

"You again!" Miss Andrew's face was contorted with rage and the realisation that for the second time Mary Poppins had bamboozled her. "It was you who made me perform like that – so shameful, so undignified! And you, you, YOU, who sent Luti away!" She pointed a large, trembling finger at the calm and smiling figure.

"Nonsense, madam, you are much mistaken," the Prime Minister broke in. "No one can force another to dance. You owe it to your own two feet, and very apt they were. As for Miss Poppins, a respectable well-behaved young woman, always so busy with her charges, could such a one gallivant about, dispatching cooks – or for that matter, chemists – to somewhere in the South Seas? Certainly not. It's unthinkable!"

Jane and Michael looked at each other. The unthinkable, they knew, had been thought. It had, indeed, recently happened. And Luti was on his way to his homeland.

"Everyone needs his own home," said Mary Poppins calmly. And she twirled the perambulator round and sent it speeding homewards.

"And I need mine," cried Miss Andrew wildly, flinging herself against Binnacle's front door.

"Well, you've got one here," said Binnacle. "Unless –" he smiled a terrible pirate smile – "unless you'd prefer Number Eighteen."

"Oh, never, never! Not without Luti!" Miss Andrew buried her face in her hands. And before she knew it, Binnacle and the Prime Minister – who was still holding the medicine bag – had hustled her into the house.

"Well, she's safely in port," said Admiral Boom. "They'll put her on an even keel."

And, taking Mrs Boom's arm, he allowed her to lead him away.

It was growing dark when Mr Banks, coming along the Lane, glanced at Binnacle's front window and beheld a curious sight. In a small room, clean and bare as the deck of a ship, sat Miss Andrew in the only chair, looking like somebody who has been shipwrecked. An empty glass stood on a table nearby and beside her, squatting on his haunches, was Binnacle, absorbed in something she was reading aloud – an activity that, from the look on her face, filled her with rage and disgust.

And, in the doorway, intently listening, was no less a person than the Prime Minister. The Head of the State in Cherry Tree Lane concerning himself with the goings-on in the home of an ex-pirate!

Amazed, Mr Banks took off his hat. "Can I be of service, Prime Minister? Is anything amiss?"

"Oh, Banks, my dear fellow, such tribulations! The lady whom you see inside has vacated Number Eighteen because her companion – a cook or a chemist, I'm not sure which – has apparently deserted her. And Binnacle, the Admiral's servant, has taken her to live with him on two important conditions – one, that she dance the Sailor's Hornpipe and the other, that she read to him. Well, she has danced, though unwillingly, and now she is reading aloud."

"I am flabbergasted!" said Mr Banks. "Miss Andrew dancing! Luti gone! I think you should know, Prime Minister, that that companion was neither a cook nor a chemist, but a boy hardly taller than my daughter Jane, who was brought by Miss Andrew from the Southern Seas."

"A child! Good Heavens, we must get the police! A lost boy must be searched for."

"I wouldn't advise it, Prime Minister. The police might frighten him. Give him just a little more time. He's a bright lad. He will find his way."

"We-ell, if you think so. You know them better than I."

"I do, indeed. Miss Andrew was once my governess. And she's known as the Holy Terror. The boy has had a lucky escape."

"Ha! Well, it's Binnacle now who's the Holy Terror. He has given her cold porridge to eat, made her drink various medicines mixed together in a single glass, and he won't let her read to him anything but copies – new or old – of *Fizzo*!"

"*Fizzo!* But that's a comic, surely. And Miss Andrew is a learnt woman. Having to read comics aloud will simply horrify her. Perhaps it will even drive her mad."

"Well, I happen to like them, Banks. I get so weary of

making Laws that I find *Fizzo* quite restful. We have just had *Tiger Tim and the Tortoise* and are now in the middle of *Sam's Adventure*. So, excuse me, please, my dear fellow. I must hear how he and Gwendolyn manage to deal with the Dragon."

"Oh, of course!" said Mr Banks politely.

And, leaving the Prime Minister craning his head to catch the story, he hurried home full of the evening's news.

Number Eighteen, as he passed it, had something of its old friendly look and Miss Lark's dogs were busily sniffing at something under the hedge. They could smell the old bones they had given Luti and, since he seemed to have gone away, they were anxious to retrieve them. Why leave such treasures for other dogs?

"I have news for you," Mr Banks exclaimed, as Mrs Banks met him at the door. "The sensation of the year, my dear! Luti is no longer with us and Miss Andrew has left Next Door and gone to live with Binnacle."

Mrs Banks gave an astonished shriek and collapsed upon a chair.

"Luti lost? Oh, that poor dear child! Shouldn't we go and look for him? So young and in a strange land."

"Oh, Luti has a good head on his shoulders. He's probably made his way to the docks and stowed away on some trading ship. It's Miss Andrew I'm thinking about. She kept that boy like a bird in a cage and now she's a bird in a cage herself, reading stories from *Fizzo*."

"*Fizzo*? Miss Andrew? I can't believe it." It was Mrs Banks' turn to be flabbergasted.

Mr Banks was almost dancing with joy. He was thinking that now his astronomer would soon be in his old haunts again, his telescope turned to the sky. He did not yet know that Next Door's invisible dwellers were already back in their places – the Grandmother, the chess companions, Admiral Boom's brave sea captain, Mrs Boom's quiet child, Mrs Banks' friendly friend, the Sleeping Beauty, Gobbo. Nor did he realise that even the nettles had begun to sprout in the garden again.

"Think of it!" he cried with delight. "Number Eighteen empty again and with luck we'll keep it so!"

"But, George, shouldn't we think of Miss Andrew? Will she be able to endure such a life?"

"No, my dear, I'm sure she won't. It's my belief that Binnacle will wake up one morning and find himself deserted – no one to read aloud to him. Miss Andrew, as we know, has a mind of her own. She's a learnt woman and a born teacher. She'll skip off somewhere, I'll be bound. Last time it was to the South. Perhaps she'll make her way Northwards and find an Eskimo, heaven help him! You mark my words, the Lane will have seen the last of her sooner than you think."

"Well, I hope so," murmured Mrs Banks. "We have had enough of that terrible snoring. Michael!" She broke off at the sight of a figure in pyjamas perched on the banisters. "You ought to be in bed!"

"And what do you think you're doing?" asked his father. "Trying to climb up the banisters?"

"I'm being a pirate," Michael panted, attempting to pull himself higher.

"Well, no one, not even a pirate, can climb *up* banisters. It's against the laws of nature. And by the way – I'm sorry to have to tell you this – Luti has gone away. We won't be seeing him again, I'm afraid."

"I know," said Michael – knowing too, though he did not say so, that Someone *had* climbed the banisters. Someone, in fact, who was not far away.

"Really!" said Mr Banks testily. "I can't think how it so often happens that my children seem to know what's afoot before I get a hint of it. Be off with you, on your two feet, like any civilised being."

Michael went unwillingly. He did not like being civilised.

At the top of the stairs Mary Poppins was waiting, a blue-clad statue with an arm outstretched that pointed to his bed.

"Oh, not again, please, Mary Poppins. I'm tired of going to bed every night."

"The night is for sleeping," she said primly. "So, in with you, spit-spot. And you too, if you please, Jane."

For Jane, holding Luti's coconut, was kneeling on the window-seat watching the full moon sailing the sky low down on the horizon. There was somebody there, though she could not see him, for whom no night was for sleeping.

"And I'll take care of that. Thank you!" Mary Poppins took the coconut and glanced at the carved smiling face that seemed to repeat, though wordlessly, Luti's phrase of, "Peace and blessings!".

She placed it on the mantelpiece and as she did so her image looked at her from the mirror and the two exchanged a nod of approval.

"But I wanted to watch and wake," grumbled Michael.

To his surprise Mary Poppins said nothing. She merely placed a chair by his bed and with a wide dramatic gesture invited him to sit down.

He did so, full of determination. He too would see Luti on his way.

But soon his eyes began to close. He propped them open with his fingers. But then he yawned, an enormous yawn that seemed to swallow him up.

"I'd better do it tomorrow," he said, and rolled sideways into the bed that Mary Poppins, with a look that said more than words, was turning down for him.

"Tomorrow never comes," said Jane. "When you wake up it's always today." And she too climbed into bed.

They lay there, watching Mary Poppins making her usual whirlwind round, tucking in Annabel and the Twins, pushing the rocking-horse into his corner, taking things out of pockets, folding up the clothes. As she came to Michael's sailor blouse, she tossed the mouth organ to him.

He decided to give it another try, blowing in and blowing out, but again the mouth organ was silent.

"It still won't work for me," he said, "and it wouldn't for the Man-in-the-Moon. I wonder, Mary Poppins, why it worked for you when you played the Sailor's Hornpipe?"

She favoured him with a quick blue glance. "I wonder!"

she said mockingly, and went on being a whirlwind.

Jane too would have liked to watch and wake, but she knew that she could not do it. So she lay still, thinking of Luti – picturing the singing, leaping figure, wrapped in the scarf of woollen roses, careering across the sky. For Luti too, the night was not for sleeping. And suddenly, she was anxious.

"Suppose, Mary Poppins," she burst out. "Suppose there are not enough clouds up there to take him all the way!" She remembered many a clear, bright night when from corner to corner of the world, there was nothing but dark blue sky. "What if he came to an empty space? How could he go further?"

"There's always a cloud about somewhere," said Mary Poppins comfortably. And she set a match to the wick of the night-light where it stood on the mantelpiece, a small and glowing likeness of the big lamp on the table. As usual, it would watch all night. And the two lamps filled the room with shadows that were themselves like clouds.

Jane felt reassured. "When the morning comes he will be at home, under the coconut palms. And we too will be at home, but under the Cherry Trees. It's different, but somehow the same."

"East. West. Home's Best," said Mary Poppins cheerfully, as she hung the parrot-headed umbrella on its accustomed hook.

"And you, Mary Poppins," Jane demanded, knowing that it was a daring question. "Where is your home – East or West? Where do you go when you're not here?"

"Everyone needs his own home – that's what you said today, remember?" Michael too was daring.

Mary Poppins stood by the table, a whirlwind no longer, her day's work over.

The glow from the big lamp lit up her face, the pink cheeks, the blue eyes, the turned-up nose.

She looked at them both reflectively while they waited, hardly breathing. Where did she come from – woodland or field, cottage or castle, mountain or sea? Would she or wouldn't she tell them?

Oh, she would! they thought, for her face was so vivid, so brimful of things that remained to be told.

Then a sparkle leapt to the blue eyes and the old, familiar secret smile greeted their eager faces.

"I'm at home," she said, "wherever I am!"

And with that, she turned out the lamp.

A.M.G.D.

Read an *extract* of the original

Mary Poppins

story...

Chapter One

East Wind

IF YOU WANT to find Cherry Tree Lane all you have to do is ask the Policeman at the crossroads. He will push his helmet slightly to one side, scratch his head thoughtfully, and then he will point his huge white-gloved finger and say: "First to your right, second to your left, sharp right again, and you're there. Good morning."

And sure enough, if you follow his directions exactly, you *will* be there – right in the middle of Cherry Tree Lane, where the houses run down one side and the Park runs down the other and the cherry-trees go dancing right down the middle.

If you are looking for Number Seventeen – and it is more than likely that you will be, for this book is all about that particular house – you will very soon find it. To begin with, it is the smallest house in the Lane. And besides that, it is the only one that is rather dilapidated and needs a coat of paint.

But Mr Banks, who owns it, said to Mrs Banks that she could have either a nice, clean, comfortable house or four children. But not both, for he couldn't afford it.

And after Mrs Banks had given the matter some consideration she came to the conclusion that she would rather have Jane, who was the eldest, and Michael, who came next, and John and Barbara, who were Twins and came last of all. So it was settled, and that was how the Banks family came to live at Number Seventeen, with Mrs Brill to cook for them, and Ellen to lay the tables, and Robertson Ay to cut the lawn and clean the knives and polish the shoes and, as Mr Banks always said, "to waste his time and my money."

And, of course, besides these there was Katie Nanna, who doesn't really deserve to come into the book at all because, at the time I am speaking of, she had just left Number Seventeen.

"Without a by your leave or a word of warning. And what am I to do?" said Mrs Banks.

"Advertise, my dear," said Mr Banks, putting on his shoes. "And I wish Robertson Ay would go without a word of warning, for he has again polished one boot and left the other untouched. I shall look very lopsided."

"That," said Mrs Banks, "is not of the least importance. You haven't told me what I'm to do about Katie Nanna."

"I don't see how you can do anything about her since she has disappeared," replied Mr Banks. "But if it were me – I mean I – well, I should get somebody to put in the *Morning Paper* the news that Jane and Michael and John and Barbara Banks (to say nothing of their mother) require the best possible

Nannie at the lowest possible wage and at once. Then I should wait and watch for the Nannies to queue up outside the front gate, and I should get very cross with them for holding up the traffic and making it necessary for me to give the policeman a shilling for putting him to so much trouble. Now I must be off. Whew, it's as cold as the North Pole. Which way is the wind blowing?"

And as he said that, Mr Banks popped his head out of the window and looked down the Lane to Admiral Boom's house at the corner. This was the grandest house in the Lane, and the Lane was very proud of it because it was built exactly like a ship. There was a flagstaff in the garden, and on the roof was a gilt weathercock shaped like a telescope.

"Ha!" said Mr Banks, drawing in his head very quickly. "Admiral's telescope says East Wind. I thought as much. There is frost in my bones. I shall wear two overcoats." And he kissed his wife absentmindedly on one side of her nose and waved to the children and went away to the City.

Now, the City was a place where Mr Banks went every day – except Sundays, of course, and Bank Holidays – and while he was there he sat on a large chair in front of a large desk and made money. All day long he worked, cutting out pennies and shillings and half-crowns and threepenny-bits. And he brought them home with him in his little black bag. Sometimes he would give some to Jane and Michael for their money-boxes, and when he couldn't spare any he would say, "The Bank is broken," and they would know he hadn't made much money that day.

Well, Mr Banks went off with his black bag, and Mrs Banks went into the drawing room and sat there all day long writing letters to the papers and begging them to send some Nannies to her at once as she was waiting; and upstairs in the Nursery, Jane and Michael watched at the window and wondered who would come. They were glad Katie Nanna had gone, for they had never liked her. She was old and fat and smelt of barley-water. Anything, they thought, would be better than Katie Nanna – if not *much* better.

When the afternoon began to die away behind the Park, Mrs Brill and Ellen came to give them their supper and to bath the Twins. And after supper Jane and Michael sat at the window watching for Mr Banks to come home, and listening to the sound of the East Wind blowing through the naked branches of the cherry trees in the Lane. The trees themselves, turning and bending in the half light, looked as though they had gone mad and were dancing their roots out of the ground.

"There he is!" said Michael, pointing suddenly to a shape that banged heavily against the gate. Jane peered through the gathering darkness.

"That's not Daddy," she said. "It's somebody else."

Then the shape, tossed and bent under the wind, lifted the latch of the gate, and they could see that it belonged to a woman, who was holding her hat on with one hand and carrying a bag in the other. As they watched, Jane and Michael saw a curious thing happen. As soon as the shape was inside the gate the wind seemed to catch her up into the air and fling her at the house. It was as though it had flung her first at the gate, waited for her to open it, and then lifted and thrown her, bag and all, at the front door. The watching children heard a terrific bang, and as she landed the whole house shook.

"How funny! I've never seen that happen before," said Michael.

"Let's go and see who it is!" said Jane, and taking Michael's arm she drew him away from the window, through the Nursery and out on to the landing. From there they always had a good view of anything that happened in the front hall.

Presently they saw their Mother coming out of the drawing room with a visitor following her. Jane and Michael could see that the newcomer had shiny black hair – "Rather like a wooden Dutch doll," whispered Jane. And that she was thin, with large feet and hands, and small, rather peering blue eyes.

"You'll find that they are very nice children," Mrs Banks was saying.

Michael's elbow gave a sharp dig at Jane's ribs.

"And that they give no trouble at all," continued Mrs Banks uncertainly, as if she herself didn't really believe what she was saying. They heard the visitor sniff as though *she* didn't either.

"Now, about references—" Mrs Banks went on.

"Oh, I make it a rule never to give references," said the other firmly. Mrs Banks stared.

"But I thought it was usual," she said. "I mean – I understood people always did."

"A very old-fashioned idea, to *my* mind," Jane and Michael heard the stern voice say. "*Very* old-fashioned. *Quite* out of date, as you might say."

Now, if there was one thing Mrs Banks did not like, it was to be thought old-fashioned. She just couldn't bear it. So she said quickly:

"Very well, then. We won't bother about them. I only asked, of course, in case *you* – er – required it. The nursery is upstairs—" And she led the way towards the staircase, talking all the time, without stopping once. And because she was doing that Mrs Banks did not notice what was happening behind her, but Jane and Michael, watching from the top landing, had an excellent view of the extraordinary thing the visitor now did.

Certainly she followed Mrs Banks upstairs, but not in the usual way. With her large bag in her hands she slid gracefully *up* the banisters, and arrived at the landing at the same time as Mrs Banks. Such a thing, Jane and Michael knew, had never been done before. Down, of course, for they had often done it themselves. But up – never! They gazed curiously at the strange new visitor.

"Well, that's all settled, then." A sigh of relief came from the children's Mother.

"Quite. As long as *I'm* satisfied," said the other, wiping her nose with a large red and white bandanna handkerchief.

"Why, children," said Mrs Banks, noticing them suddenly, "what are you doing there? This is your new nurse, Mary Poppins. Jane, Michael, say how do you do! And these" – she waved her hand at the babies in their cots – "are the Twins."

Mary Poppins regarded them steadily, looking from one to the other as though she were making up her mind whether she liked them or not.

"Will we do?" said Michael.

"Michael, don't be naughty," said his Mother.

Mary Poppins continued to regard the four children searchingly. Then, with a long, loud sniff that seemed to indicate that she had made up her mind, she said:

"I'll take the position."

"For all the world," as Mrs Banks said to her husband later, "as though she were doing us a signal honour."

"Perhaps she is," said Mr Banks, putting his nose round the corner of the newspaper for a moment and then withdrawing it very quickly.

When their Mother had gone, Jane and Michael edged towards Mary Poppins, who stood, still as a post, with her hands folded in front of her.

"How did you come?" Jane asked. "It looked just as if the wind blew you here."

"It did," said Mary Poppins briefly. And she proceeded to unwind her muffler from her neck and to take off her hat, which she hung on one of the bedposts.

As it did not seem as though Mary Poppins was going to say any more – though she sniffed a great deal – Jane, too, remained silent. But when she bent down to undo her bag, Michael could not restrain himself.

"What a funny bag!" he said, pinching it with his fingers.

"Carpet," said Mary Poppins, putting her key in the lock.

"To carry carpets in, you mean?"

"No. Made of."

"Oh," said Michael. "I see." But he didn't – quite.

By this time the bag was open, and Jane and Michael were more than surprised to find it was completely empty.

"Why," said Jane, "there's nothing in it!"

"What do you mean – nothing?" demanded Mary Poppins, drawing herself up and looking as though she had been insulted. "Nothing in it, did you say?"

And with that she took out from the empty bag a starched white apron and tied it round her waist. Next she unpacked a large cake of Sunlight Soap, a toothbrush, a packet of hairpins, a bottle of scent, a small folding armchair and a box of throat lozenges.

Jane and Michael stared.

"But I *saw*," whispered Michael. "I'm sure it was empty."

"Hush!" said Jane, as Mary Poppins took out a large bottle labelled "One Teaspoon to be Taken at Bedtime."

A spoon was attached to the neck of the bottle, and into this Mary Poppins poured a dark crimson fluid.

"Is that your medicine?" enquired Michael, looking very interested.

"No, yours," said Mary Poppins, holding out the spoon to him. Michael stared. He wrinkled up his nose. He began to protest.

"I don't want it. I don't need it. I won't!"

But Mary Poppins' eyes were fixed upon him, and Michael suddenly discovered that you could not look at Mary Poppins and disobey her. There was something strange and extraordinary about her – something that was frightening and at the same time most exciting. The spoon came nearer. He held his breath, shut his eyes and gulped. A delicious taste ran round his mouth. He turned his tongue in it. He swallowed, and a happy smile ran round his face.

"Strawberry ice," he said ecstatically. "More, more, more!"

But Mary Poppins, her face as stern as before, was pouring out a dose for Jane. It ran into the spoon, silvery, greeny, yellowy. Jane tasted it.

"Lime-juice cordial," she said, sliding her tongue deliciously over her lips. But when she saw Mary Poppins moving towards the Twins with the bottle Jane rushed at her.

"Oh, no – please. They're too young. It wouldn't be good for them. Please!"

Mary Poppins, however, took no notice, but with a warning, terrible glance at Jane, tipped the spoon towards John's mouth. He lapped at it eagerly, and by the few drops that were spilt on his bib, Jane and Michael could tell that the substance in the spoon this time was milk. Then Barbara had her share, and she gurgled and licked the spoon twice.

Mary Poppins then poured out another dose and solemnly took it herself.

"Rum punch," she said, smacking her lips and corking the bottle.

Jane's eyes and Michael's popped with astonishment, but they were not given much time to wonder, for Mary Poppins, having put the miraculous bottle on the mantelpiece, turned to them.

"Now," she said, "spit-spot into bed." And she began to undress them. They noticed that whereas buttons and hooks had needed all sorts of coaxing from Katie Nanna, for Mary Poppins they flew apart almost at a look. In less than a minute they found themselves in bed and watching, by the dim light from the night-light, the rest of Mary Poppins' unpacking being performed.

From the carpet bag she took out seven flannel nightgowns, four cotton ones, a pair of boots, a set of dominoes, two bathing-caps and a postcard album. Last of all came a folding camp-bedstead with blankets and eiderdown complete, and this she set down between John's cot and Barbara's.

Jane and Michael sat hugging themselves and watching. It was all so surprising that they could find nothing to say. But they knew, both of them, that something strange and wonderful had happened at Number Seventeen, Cherry Tree Lane.

Mary Poppins, slipping one of the flannel nightgowns over her head, began to undress underneath it as though it were a tent. Michael, charmed by this strange new arrival, unable to keep silent any longer, called to her.

"Mary Poppins," he cried, "you'll never leave us, will you?"

There was no reply from under the nightgown. Michael could not bear it.

"You won't leave us, will you?" he called anxiously.

Mary Poppins' head came out of the top of the nightgown. She looked very fierce.

"One word more from that direction," she said threateningly, "and I'll call the Policeman."

"I was only saying," began Michael, meekly, "that we hoped

you wouldn't be going away soon—" He stopped, feeling very red and confused.

Mary Poppins stared from him to Jane in silence. Then she sniffed.

"I'll stay till the wind changes," she said shortly, and she blew out her candle and got into bed.

"That's all right," said Michael, half to himself and half to Jane. But Jane wasn't listening. She was thinking about all that had happened, and wondering...

And that is how Mary Poppins came to live at Number Seventeen, Cherry Tree Lane. And although they sometimes found themselves wishing for the quieter, more ordinary days when Katie Nanna ruled the household, everybody, on the whole, was glad of Mary Poppins' arrival. Mr Banks was glad because, as she arrived by herself and did not hold up the traffic, he had not had to tip the Policeman. Mrs Banks was glad because she was able to tell everybody that *her* children's nurse was so fashionable that she didn't believe in giving references. Mrs Brill and Ellen were glad because they could drink strong cups of tea all day in the kitchen and no longer needed to preside at nursery suppers. Robertson Ay was glad, too, because Mary Poppins had only one pair of shoes, and those she polished herself.

But nobody ever knew what Mary Poppins felt about it, for Mary Poppins never told anything...

Discover more about

Mary Poppins

and P. L. Travers...

Postscript by Brian Sibley

"If you are looking for autobiographical facts," P. L. Travers once wrote, "*Mary Poppins* is the story of my life." This seems rather unlikely, when you consider that Mary Poppins goes inside a chalk pavement picture, slides up banisters, arranges tea-parties on the ceiling and has a carpet bag which is both empty and – *at the same time* – contains many strange but useful objects. And yet memories of people and events from her life *did* find their way into the Mary Poppins stories – not that most people were aware of that. Even those of us who were her friends knew little about her private life.

One thing we did know was that, as a child growing up in Australia, she had fallen in love with the fairy-tales, myths and legends from which she later borrowed some of the ideas and images found in her own books. Her passion for reading naturally led her to become a storyteller, beginning her writing career as a journalist and poet some years before she wrote her first full-length novel. It was in one of her earliest stories – written before she left Australia for Britain in 1924 – that a character appeared named Mary Poppins. She was neither magical nor particularly memorable, but the author had found a name that she would one day give to somebody else…

That "somebody" blew into Pamela Travers' imagination rather as Mary Poppins herself blew into Cherry Tree Lane. The author was staying in an old thatched manor in Sussex and was ill in bed. She once described it to me: "The idea of the person came to me and, in that halfway s being well and ill, I began to write abo

So, some parts of Mary Poppins came to Pamela from out of the blue; others were memories of her earlier life when she was growing up on an Australian sugar plantation. Bertha (or maybe she was called Bella – Pamela could never quite remember!), one of the family's Irish servants, was a marvellous character whose pride and joy was a parrot-headed umbrella. "Whenever Bertha was going out," Pamela told me, "the umbrella would be carefully taken out of tissue paper and off she would go, looking terribly stylish. But, as soon as she came back, the umbrella would be wrapped up in tissue paper once more."

Like Mary Poppins, Bertha also had a number of fascinating relatives whom she would visit. Pamela recalled: "She would come back and tell us wonderful stories... But no – she wouldn't quite tell. She'd just *hint*: 'If you could know what happened to me cousin's brother-in-law...' And when you'd opened your ears and your eyes – *and* your mouth – waiting for more, she would say: 'Ah, well, then, it's not for the ears of children...' And I would wonder what *were* those things that were not for the ears of children."

Some children's writers – maybe because they worry about what is suitable for the ears of children – talk down to their readers. Not P. L. Travers. "Nobody writes for children really," she'd say. "You're writing to make *yourself* laugh, or *yourself* cry; if you write for children, you've lost them." Her readers proved her right, and wrote to the author in their thousands, often asking the same questions: Where did Mary Poppins come from? Why did she go? And *where* did she go?

From every point of the compass – and Mary Poppins knew all about compasses! – children would send their letters, carefully written in large, round writing, punctuating their demands for answers with words of praise and, occasionally, complaint. When, at the end of *Mary Poppins Opens the Door*, the heroine flew away for the third time, a boy (who wasn't the world's best speller) wrote mournfully: "You should not have done that, Madum, you have made the children cry." Pamela treasured that letter, and replied: "I am not surprised. I cried myself, when I wrote it down."

The only rule Pamela had about writing was that there were no set rules. She wrote her stories, she said, "because they were there to be written". The actual business of catching ideas and getting them on paper was a mysterious and lonely process; and yet, as she would explain, "you can do it anywhere, any time – when you're out at the shops buying a pound of butter – still it goes on. Even if you forget your idea by the time you get home, you wait a little and then it will come back if it wants to."

And the ideas did come back, or maybe she had never forgotten them? "Spit spot into bed" was a favourite phrase of hers, and other bits of Mary Poppins' characte~~r~~stina Saraset, whom eve~~ry~~dy spinster aun~~t~~ass". She was a crisp, no~~~~ called "~~~~ a sharp tongue and a heart ~~~~ wor~~~~

like Mary Poppins, was given to making "a curious convulsion in her nose that was something between a snort and a sniff".

When Pamela once suggested to her aunt that she might write about her, the elderly lady replied: "What! You put me in a book! I trust you will never so far forget yourself as to do anything so vulgarly disgusting!" This indignant response was followed up with a contemptuous, "Sniff, sniff!" Doesn't this sound just like Mary Poppins speaking? Equally, it might have been P. L. Travers herself, who said something very similar to me when I rashly suggested one day that I might write her life story!

I received a similar reaction – the severe look and the sniff! – when I once wondered aloud whether Mary Poppins was based on a real person. After all, the character is very real to a great many people. Pamela herself had once told me how a harassed mother of three had written to ask for Mary Poppins' address, adding: "Because if she has really left the Banks family, couldn't she come to me?" In reply to my question, however, all Pamela would say was, "Well? Have you ever met anyone like Mary Poppins?" Taken aback by her brusque tone, I was silent for a moment, then summoned up my courage and said that I hadn't but that I rather wished I had.

What I should have said was what I knew in my heart, which was, that I have met someone very like Mary Poppins – and that is you..."

Mary Poppins

P. L. Travers was born in 1899, in Maryborough in Queensland, Australia, one of three sisters. She was a keen reader, particularly of all kinds of myths and legends, but before long she moved on to reading her mother's library books (which involved sneaking into her room while she was asleep!).

Pamela deliberately kept her life very private. She lived for a while in Ireland and London, and travelled frequently to America, where she was made writer in residence to both Smith and Radcliffe Colleges in Massachusetts. She also received an honorary doctorate from Chatham College, Pittsburgh.

Although she worked as a secretary, a dancer and an actress, writing was P. L. Travers' real love, and for many years she was a journalist. It was while she was recuperating from a serious illness that she wrote *Mary Poppins* – "to while away the days, but also to put down something that had been in my mind for a long time", she said. She received an OBE in 1977, and died in 1996.

All about...

P. L. Travers

P. L. Travers real name is Helen Lyndon Goff; she chose a pen name to disguise her gender

The author was fascinated with astronomy

Travers knew the author and poet T. S. Eliot

According to P. L. Travers, "All the best fan letters come from men or boys (because) men really put you on the spot"

Pamela Lyndon Travers was Australian, but would always say she was a "Citizen of the British Empire"

As well as a writer, the author was a journalist, poet, dancer and actress

Mary Shepard

Mary Shepard's father was E.H. Shepard, who illustrated Winnie the Pooh and The Wind in the Willows

Shepard drew an image of herself and P. L. Travers in the "Balloons and Balloons!" chapter in the book *Mary Poppins Comes Back*. They are floating together with magic balloons with other characters from the book

The Illustrator collaborated with P. L. Travers for over fifty years

Nanny Knows Best

In Victorian times, children of upper and upper middle class families would have been placed in the charge of a nanny and governess. The children would have seen more of their nanny than their parents and Nanny would ensure they had a rigorous upbringing and behaved appropriately at all times.

How would you feel about having to live by these strict rules?

Exercise
A brisk walk every day, or several times a day,
will improve a child's constitution

Diet
Good, healthy food with lots of fruit and vegetables

Appearance
Clean hands, nails and face at all times; teeth and hair brushed.
Neat clothes and hair ribbons (for girls)

Manners
A child should always stand up when an adult comes into
the room and most importantly, a child should be seen
and not heard!

Parents
A child will see their parents for one hour, before bedtime.
Best behaviour must be displayed at all times